Eye on Crime

"Frank, Joe!" a voice boomed suddenly. The players all looked at the dugout entrance, which was filled by the form of their coach.

"Yes, Coach," Frank said.

"You two get on over to the locker room. Somebody there to see you."

"What's up?" Joe asked. "The game's going to start soon."

"I know," the coach replied. "You two are scrubbed for the day."

Frank and Joe left the dugout and headed for the locker room. When they got there, Officer Con Riley was waiting for them.

"Has there been a break in the jewelry case?" Frank asked.

"In a way," Con said. "Look, I hate to do this, but Frank and Joe Hardy, you are both under arrest."

The Hardy Boys Mystery Stories

#88 Tricky Business
#89 The Sky Blue Frame
#96 Wipeout
#104 Tricks of the Trade
#105 The Smoke Screen Mystery
#107 Panic on Gull Island
#110 The Secret of Sigma Seven
#114 The Case of the Counterfeit Criminals
#116 Rock 'n' Roll Renegades
#123 The Robot's Revenge
#124 Mystery with a Dangerous Beat
#128 Day of the Dinosaur
#132 Maximum Challenge
#133 Crime in the Kennel
#136 The Cold Cash Caper
#138 The Alaskan Adventure
#139 The Search for the Snow Leopard
#140 Slam Dunk Sabotage
#141 The Desert Thieves
#142 Lost in Gator Swamp
#143 The Giant Rat of Sumatra
#144 The Secret of Skeleton Reef
#145 Terror at High Tide
#146 The Mark of the Blue Tattoo
#147 Trial and Terror
#148 The Ice-Cold Case
#149 The Chase for the Mystery Twister
#150 The Crisscross Crime
#151 The Rocky Road to Revenge
#152 Danger in the Extreme
#153 Eye on Crime
#154 The Caribbean Cruise Caper

Available from MINSTREL Books

EYE ON CRIME

FRANKLIN W. DIXON

Published by POCKET BOOKS
New York London Toronto Sydney Tokyo Singapore

This book is a work of fiction. Names, characters, places and incidents are products of the author's imagination or are used fictitiously. Any resemblance to actual events or locales or persons, living or dead, is entirely coincidental.

A MINSTREL PAPERBACK *Original*

A Minstrel Book published by
POCKET BOOKS, a division of Simon & Schuster Inc.
1230 Avenue of the Americas, New York, NY 10020

Front cover illustration by John Youssi

Produced by Mega-Books, Inc.

ISBN: 0-671-02174-5

First Minstrel Books printing December 1998

10 9 8 7 6 5 4 3 2

Printed in the U.S.A.

Contents

For orders other than by individual consumers, Pocket Books grants a discount on the purchase of **10 or more** copies of single titles for special markets or premium use. For further details, please write to the Vice-President of Special Markets, Pocket Books, 1633 Broadway, New York, NY 10019-6785, 8th Floor.

For information on how individual consumers can place orders, please write to Mail Order Department, Simon & Schuster Inc., 200 Old Tappan Road, Old Tappan, NJ 07675.

1 Somebody Gets Chosen

"So then Callie and I said, 'Sure, we'll go out with you guys. It's not like our boyfriends ever pay any attention to us.' "

Joe Hardy nodded his head and grunted, but he never took his eyes off the newspaper his older brother, Frank, was holding to look at his girlfriend, Iola Morton. The four teenagers were sitting together in the audience at WBAY, Bayport's local television studio. They had come to the studio after school to watch the Thursday afternoon taping of *Monty Mania*, a comedy variety show that was fast becoming one of the hottest programs on syndicated television.

"It's useless," Iola said to Callie Shaw. "Something more important than us has the dynamic duo's attention." Iola gently pushed on Joe's shoulder.

"Huh, uh, hey," Joe said, looking up from the newspaper. Joe rubbed his shoulder even though the punch hadn't hurt at all.

"Hey, Joe," Frank said. "It says here—" But before Frank could finish his sentence, Callie had grabbed the newspaper from his hands.

"It says here," Callie said, "that it's pretty rude to be out with a couple of friends and have your head buried in the *Bayport Times.*"

Frank looked at Callie. "Oh, I'm sorry," he said sincerely. He gently nudged his brother with his elbow.

"Yeah," Joe said. "I'm sorry."

"It was wrong of us to ignore you like that," Frank said. "It's just that we got caught up reading today's front-page news while we were waiting for you two to get here."

"And this excuses your poor behavior now?" Iola asked.

The four friends sat in silence for a moment. Frank and Joe both eyed the newspaper, which was still clasped in Callie's hand.

"Ummm," Joe groaned sheepishly.

"Oh, all right," Callie said with a shrug of her shoulders. She handed the newspaper back to Frank. The blond-haired Hardy quickly unfolded the *Bayport Times* and straightened out the front page.

"What's so important in today's news, anyway?" Callie leaned over to get a better look at the headline.

"You had to ask," Iola said, rolling her eyes. Then she, too, leaned in to read over Joe's shoulder.

"Something major involving some guys from Shoreham High School," Frank said.

"Who?" Iola asked.

"Roberto Rojas and Pepper Wingfoot," Joe responded.

"Whoa," Callie said. "Those names sound familiar."

"Sure do," Frank answered. "They both play on Shoreham's baseball team."

"So what did they do?" Callie asked.

"*Allegedly* do," Frank responded. "They were arrested for robbing the Bayport Jewelry Exchange last night."

"That's a felony!" Iola exclaimed.

"Yeah," Joe replied. Then he added, "What do you mean by 'allegedly,' Frank? They were caught on video by the store's security system. They're nailed."

"Not necessarily, Joe," Frank replied. "Rojas and Wingfoot claim that they're innocent."

"Doesn't every criminal?" Joe asked snidely.

"Well, in this country you *are* innocent until proven guilty," Callie said.

"So how much did they get away with?" Iola asked.

"Allegedly got away with," Frank said. "It says here nearly one million dollars' worth of jewels, which have yet to be recovered."

"Uh-oh," Callie said. "I don't like that tone in your voice."

"Yeah," Iola continued for her friend. "You're using words like 'allegedly' and 'yet to be recovered.' Are you two planning to get involved?"

"Involved!" Callie fixed Frank with a glare. "The last time you guys got involved in a case, Iola and I didn't see you for weeks."

"Are you getting jealous?" Joe asked. He chuckled. "Do you miss us that much?"

Iola snickered. "Don't get too full of yourself, Joe. We just get tired of being left behind while you go off hunting down criminals or foiling robberies."

"Or stopping kidnappings," Callie added, "or rescuing lost puppies, or—"

Frank interrupted. "You do sound jealous," he said. "Maybe you two would like to do some crime solving. You know, get in on the action."

"Our lives have plenty of action," Callie said.

"That's right," Iola said. "You two are the supersleuths, not us."

"Methinks the ladies doth protest too much," Frank said, flamboyantly gesturing with his arms. He looked at his brother and cocked an eyebrow.

"Methinks you doth be right," Joe said. "'Tis certainly jealousy." The two young men grinned.

Callie and Iola sneered at the brothers, putting on their grimmest we-don't-find-you-funny looks.

"We said—" Iola began. But just then the stage lights came on, signaling that the show was about to begin. With the stage illuminated, the audience could see that a four-piece band had set up their equipment on the far left of the set. When the lights came up, the band began to play some funky jazz.

"Good afternoon, folks," a man said as he walked out from behind a curtain and onto the stage. He wore a pullover shirt and slacks, and his blond hair was flattened by an audio headset.

"I'm Josh Symkins, assistant producer here at *Monty Mania.* Most shows get a comedian to come out to warm up the crowd, but you folks just get me. And trust me, even my own mother doesn't think I'm funny."

The audience laughed politely and clapped. The band's drummer gave several quick taps on his snare drum.

"Thanks," Symkins said. "Anyway, I'm out here to tell you some of the rules and to ask some favors."

"Rules?" Joe mumbled under his breath.

"First of all," Symkins said, "if any person here has a heart condition, high blood pressure, or an oenail, be sure not to laugh too hard. My wanted a doctor, but she got me instead.”

audience gave a genuine laugh to the assis- producer this time.

Seriously, though, we here at *Monty Mania* need a favor. We can’t afford to hire any other performers except for Monty and the wonderful Billy Thompson Band to entertain you.” Symkins pointed over to the band, which acknowledged him with a short fanfare.

“So,” the assistant producer continued, “we need you to help entertain yourselves. During the taping, Monty will ask for volunteers from the audience to come down to the stage to take part in the show. So again, heart patients; stressed-out, overworked grumps; and those with painful boo-boos need not apply. Monty likes to put his performers through their paces, and sometimes that means some hard work for anybody brave enough to be on television. So, are any of you brave enough?”

The audience filled the sound stage with hoots, whoops, and enthusiastic applause.

“Oh, one more thing you potential volunteers should know,” Symkins added. “Odds are, if you come down here, you will get hypnotized. After all, before he broke into television, Monty was a hypnotist of no repute. Now that he’s famous, he wants to make you famous, too. So, if you have any secrets you don’t want revealed to the rest of the world, stay in your seats. If you come down here, Monty may just catch you with your pants down."

The audience laughed once more. Symkins raised his hands to stop the applause.

"One more 'one more thing,'" he added. "Those who do participate in the show will not be returning to their seats. After you star up here, you have to meet with the studio's lawyers back there." Symkins pointed offstage.

"You'll be required to sign some legal mumbo jumbo releasing the studio and its officials from any harm or liability that may result from your appearance here. But for your troubles, you'll get to meet Monty after the show for autographs and pictures, and we'll send you on your way with a complimentary videotape of your performance."

Josh Symkins began to walk back behind the curtain. "So," he said over his shoulder, "anyone still brave enough?"

"Wow!" Iola exclaimed as Symkins left the stage. "We should all volunteer to be on the show!"

"That's a great idea," Callie said.

"Except," Joe said, "we're all supposed to meet Chet and Tony right after the show. The AP made it sound like whoever volunteers would have to stick around for a while."

"Oh, yeah," Callie said, a little disappointed.

"Chet's my brother," Iola said. "He won't mind if we're late."

"How about this," Frank said. "We came in two cars. If you girls want to volunteer for the show and actually get on, then Joe and I can go ahead and meet Chet and Tony and you can join us later. That way they won't be sitting around wondering where we all are."

"Sounds good to me," Iola said.

Just then the Billy Thompson Band drowned out the crowd's chatter with a rousing bass beat. As the music built, a booming voice introduced Monty Andrews. The flamboyant comedian's straight blond hair flapped against the collar of his red sports coat as he jogged from behind the curtain onto the stage. Monty held up his hands to acknowledge the audience's enthusiasm for his appearance.

"Okay, folks," Monty said as the applause diminished. "I see we have a lot of kids in the audience. That gives me an idea. How about an all-teenagers *Monty Mania?*" The audience burst out with hoots and clapping.

"All right then," Monty said. He grabbed a microphone from its stand and made his way into the audience.

"What's your name?" he asked, leaning over to put the mike in front of a teenage boy.

"Uh." The boy hesitated.

"Ehhhh. Wrong!" Monty shouted. He pulled the mike away from the embarrassed teenager and scanned the seats. His eyes locked on the enthusiastic smiles and waves of Callie and Iola.

"Whoa!" Monty said as he bounded across the aisle and up the steps to where Callie and Iola sat with Frank and Joe.

"And what are your names?" he asked, putting the microphone in front of the girls.

"Callie Shaw!"

"And Iola Morton!"

"You two want to make some television?"

"You bet!" the girls shouted in unison.

Monty pointed at Frank and Joe. "Are these your boyfriends?"

"Most of the time," Iola said.

"What are your names?"

"Frank and Joe Hardy," Joe answered.

"Well, Frank and Joe Hardy, mind if I steal your girlfriends?"

"Seems to be the theme of the day," Frank answered.

Monty and the audience laughed. "Well, then, Callie and Iola, you are mine!"

Monty began to run down the stairs back to the stage. He motioned the two girls to follow him.

When the three had gathered on the stage, Monty explained what he wanted to do.

"I haven't hypnotized anybody since I talked a traffic cop out of a speeding ticket this morning. So, let's start with that."

Monty quickly went through his hypnotism routine, putting both girls into a deep trance.

"Under hypnosis," Monty explained to the audience, "you can get people to do things they normally would never do in public. However, you can never get somebody to go against their true nature, so we won't be able to get these two to do anything that isn't already hidden deep inside of them. Let's see if they're really under."

Monty pointed out into the audience.

"Frank and Joe Hardy, what would you like your girlfriends to do? Within reason, of course."

Frank and Joe looked at each other. "Oh, I know," Joe said. "Ask them what their favorite animals are and then have them become those animals."

"A standard request," Monty answered, "but always good for a laugh."

The hypnotist asked Callie and Iola what their favorite animals were, and soon Callie was purring like a kitten, romping around the stage after an imaginary ball of string, while Iola galloped around like a horse romping through the woods.

When Monty corralled the two girls, he had them stop being animals.

"Now, as if that wasn't embarrassing enough, let's see what sort of dark secrets you may be hiding."

2 Iola and Callie Tell the Truth

"Okay, Callie and Iola," Monty Andrews continued. "We know what sort of animals you like to be, but what about humans? What people out there would you really want to be like for a short while?"

As soon as Monty asked the question, the studio fell silent. Callie and Iola both stared straight into the audience. Then, in unison, they pointed to where their boyfriends were sitting.

"The people we'd want to be like are Frank and Joe Hardy," the girls said, as if they spoke with one voice.

Frank and Joe stared in amazement at their girlfriends for a second, then looked at each other in shock. The audience burst out with laughter.

"Well, it seems like a lot of people in our studio

know who Frank and Joe Hardy are!" Monty said. "Nice to be popular, huh, boys?"

Then Monty turned to Callie and Iola. "So, you want to be just like your pals up there. That has to be the best answer of the year!"

The audience laughed and applauded. When the noise simmered down a bit, Monty continued his questioning.

"Why do you want to be like Frank and Joe Hardy?"

"Because," Iola said staring straight ahead, still under the effects of hypnosis, "they're detectives."

"Detectives?"

"Yes," Callie responded, "detectives."

"Must be an echo in here," Monty said. "What's so cool about teenage boy detectives?"

"They get to do exciting, sometimes dangerous things," Iola replied.

"They're always wrapped up in some interesting case," Callie said.

"I wonder if they're really hypnotized," Joe murmured to his brother.

"Yeah," Frank whispered. "Maybe they aren't hypnotized. They could be trying to embarrass us."

"Dangerous cases?" Monty asked. His expression was very animated with his obvious interest.

"Sometimes it's dangerous," Iola said.

"What sort of dangerous cases?"

"Robbery, kidnapping," Iola said.

"Daring rescues, sleuthing," Callie added.

Monty turned to look offstage. "Phil," he called, "could we get some sort of props out here for our guests? Something with a robbery motif."

"So, girls," Monty said turning back to his guests, "after our commercial break, I want you to show us how you would do things if you were your idols, the detective brothers named Frank and Joe Hardy."

The red light atop each camera went off, signaling that taping had ceased for the moment. The audience murmured quietly as stagehands began wheeling out props for the next part of the show. Frank and Joe looked at their girlfriends, who stood like blank-faced statues on the stage.

"Wow, that's a mindblower," Joe said to his brother.

"I'll say. Who would have thought Iola would make such a convincing horse?" Frank slapped his brother gently on the leg.

"You know what I mean," Joe replied.

"Yeah, well, let's make a pact never to hold this against them. Iola and Callie would never forgive us if we reminded them that they pretended to be us."

"Can't we rub it in just a little?"

"Not if you don't want to look for a new girlfriend," Frank answered.

Onstage, the crew set up a stanchion from which hung a door. They also wheeled out a long counter with several glass-top cases, the kind that would be found in any retail store. A second counter with a cash register was also wheeled onto the stage. Another set of stanchions was set up, this one with a window unit in it. Finally one of the stagehands handed Iola a flashlight and a screwdriver and gave Callie some rope, a roll of electrician's tape, and a flashlight.

After everything was in position, Monty got the ready sign from Josh Symkins. The red taping lights on the cameras popped back on, and Monty continued his act.

"Callie and Iola, let me set the scene," Monty said. "It's late at night, long after the rest of the world has gone to sleep, except for the Hardy Girls. Instead of being snuggled up warm in your beds, you're out working on a case. The local video store has been selling illegal copies of the latest blockbuster movie—starring me, of course. So you go to the store to look for some clues. Show us how you'd operate."

Iola and Callie immediately dropped to the floor. Staying very low to the ground, the two girls crawled over to where the fake door was placed. Very silently, they stood up next to the door as if they were trying to blend into the shadows. Iola took the screwdriver and jimmied the lock on the door.

“We would have used lock picks,” Joe murmured.

“And we never crawl,” Frank added.

Meanwhile, onstage, Callie and Iola crept silently into the video store. Both girls flicked on their flashlights and scanned a narrow beam around the room. Iola pointed to a spot on what could have been the store’s wall. Callie nodded. She slunk across the room, stopped at the spot that Iola had indicated, and ripped a piece of electrician’s tape off her roll. Callie stood on her toes and reached above her head. She took the piece of tape and spread it across something that only she and Iola could see in their hypnotized state.

“Security camera,” Frank said.

“She must have remembered that from the newspaper report on Rojas and Wingfoot,” Joe offered. Frank nodded.

Satisfied that they had foiled the security camera, Callie and Iola tiptoed over to the glass-top counter. Iola made a circle with her hands on top of the glass. Then she reached through the “hole” she had just cut in the countertop and pulled her hand back out. She smiled triumphantly at whatever she believed she had just retrieved. Meanwhile, Callie went over to the cash register. She popped behind the counter, looking for something.

“Okay,” Monty said, “they’re in and they’ve

found something. Now let's see how they handle trouble."

Monty looked at Callie and Iola. "Hardy Girls," he said, "you're doing great. But suddenly, you hear the sound of police sirens outside. You forgot to check for a silent alarm."

Both Callie and Iola got shocked expressions on their faces. But like any good detectives, they quickly regained their composure. Iola pointed to the window. Callie nodded. Iola used her screwdriver to jimmy open the window. Then Callie hung the rope outside the window. The two girls climbed through the window, holding the rope as if they needed it to lower themselves. When safely on the "street" they began to run.

"Okay, ladies, that's enough," Monty said. Callie and Iola stopped in their tracks. "Come back over to me." The girls walked over to Monty.

"Weren't they wonderful detectives?" he asked the audience. Everybody applauded. "How'd they do, Frank and Joe?"

"Oh, they were wonderful!" Joe said with mock enthusiasm.

"Yeah," Frank added, "but we never would have missed the alarm." The audience burst out laughing.

"Well, I guess it's time to snap these good-natured ladies out of their trances," Monty said. He turned to face Callie and Iola. "Okay, Hardy

Girls, when I count to three, you will no longer be hypnotized. And just to make sure you carry some of the embarrassment home with you, you'll remember everything that you did up here. One, two, three!"

Callie clasped her hands to her mouth. She laughed with embarrassment. Iola smirked up at Frank and Joe. The whole audience laughed.

"Now, if you'll just go backstage, our assistant producer will have some lovely parting gifts to give you for being such good sports. Let's give our Hardy Girls a great big round of applause!"

The audience sent Callie and Iola backstage with the sounds of hoots and clapping ringing in their ears.

Frank and Joe watched their girlfriends walk behind the curtain.

"That was great!" Joe laughed.

"Yeah," Frank said. "Except it makes the two of us a little more famous than detectives should be."

"Aww, people will forget us soon enough," Joe replied. "Then we can be good old anonymous sleuths again."

The two brothers sat together, watching the end of the show. After Monty wrapped up, Frank and Joe got up to leave. The large crowd moved sluggishly through the studio toward the exit. Frank and Joe had to wait several minutes before they could get on an elevator to take them to the ground floor. When they got to the parking lot the space next to theirs was empty.

"Didn't Callie say she parked right next to us?" Joe asked.

"Yeah, she did," Frank answered. "From what the guy said before the show, we figured they wouldn't leave until after everybody from the audience was gone."

"Hmm," Joe said. He unlocked the driver's door and got into the van. Then he leaned across the seat to unlock the passenger door for Frank. Frank climbed in and buckled his seat belt.

"Maybe they went out some backstage entrance. We did have to wait awhile for the elevator."

"That must be it," Frank replied. "They're probably already at the pizza place with Chet and Tony."

Joe turned the key in the ignition. "So let's jet."

Twenty minutes later as the hour alarm on Joe's watch chimed seven the brothers pulled up in front of their favorite pizza place, which also happened to be where Tony Prito worked as a waiter.

"I don't see Callie's car anywhere," Frank said.

The brothers got out of the van and went into the pizza place. Joe inhaled the hearty aroma of garlic and cheese.

"I love the smell of pizza when I'm hungry," he said.

"Well, I always love that smell," shouted a voice from across the room.

"Yeah, because you're always hungry, Chet," said a second voice.

Frank and Joe walked over to the table where their friends Tony Prito and Chet Morton sat. On the table between them was a pitcher of soda.

"Hi, guys," Joe said. Tony got up as the brothers sat down.

"I'll go get some more glasses and pop the pizza in the oven," Tony said.

"Shouldn't we wait until Callie and Iola get here?" Frank asked.

"Wait for food? Never," Chet replied. "But where is my sister anyway?"

Tony walked into the restaurant's kitchen.

"We're not sure," Frank said. "We thought she and Callie would be here already."

"Maybe they're too embarrassed to show up," Joe said.

"What do you mean?" Tony asked as he returned to the table. He put two more glasses on the table and filled them with soda as Frank began to tell them about Callie and Iola's television debut.

"You have got to be kidding!" Chet howled as Joe finished what Frank had begun.

"A horse!" Tony laughed and shook his head in disbelief.

"Not just that," Chet said. "The whole we-want-to-be-the-Hardy-Girls thing! It's great. I'm never going to let my sister live it down."

"Hey, wanting to be us isn't such a bad idea," Joe said.

"Well, I can't wait to see it on television next week," Tony said.

Just then Tony's boss came out of the kitchen, carrying a pan of piping-hot pizza.

"Oh, I would have gotten that," Tony said, jumping up to help with the tray.

"It's no problem," Tony's boss said. She smiled at the boys. "Just go get some plates." Tony headed for the kitchen.

"And please turn up the television," Frank said. He pointed to the television that hung on a wall bracket a few feet from where they were sitting. "*News Update* should be on in a minute."

"You and the news," the pizza shop's owner said as she put the pizza pan down on the table. "You sure do like to watch the news."

"Yeah," Chet said. "Isn't there a sitcom on or something?"

"It's good to stay informed," Frank said. "Besides, I want to catch the baseball spring-training report."

Tony returned with four plates, and the boys served themselves.

"Spring training, huh?" Chet asked. "Is it time for baseball season already?"

"Sure is," Joe replied. "And I am raring to get back out on the diamond again."

"Of course you are," Frank said. "You have a shot to break Bayport's all-time home-run record."

"And if you pitch as well as you can," Joe said to his brother, "we're sure to rack up lots of wins."

"Bayport High has a shot at the championship this year?" Tony asked.

"We sure do," Joe answered.

"All we have to do is get past Shoreham High and we're a lock," Frank said.

"Do you think you can?" Chet asked.

"If Bobby Rojas and Pepper Wingfoot end up in jail, we'll murder them."

"What are you talking about, Joe?" Chet asked.

"You really need to watch the news more," Frank said. "Rojas and Wingfoot were arrested today for robbing the Bayport Jewelry Exchange."

"Whoa, that's big-time stuff," Tony said.

"Frank, don't you mean to say 'allegedly'?" Joe chided his brother.

"What do you mean?" Chet asked.

"Frank doesn't like to convict anybody before all of the evidence is in."

"So does that mean you two plan to get involved?" Tony asked. "Or maybe the Hardy Girls are off investigating the case while we all eat pizza."

"Ha-ha," Frank said with a mock laugh. "I doubt that's where they are. And, no, we don't plan to get involved with this case. The police seem to be on top of it."

"Speaking of the girls," Joe said, "it's getting awfully late. I wonder where they could be."

"I think I'll call home to see if Iola is there," Chet said. He got up and went behind the counter to the phone.

"Good idea," Tony said.

A minute later Chet sat back down at the table. "No dice," he said.

"I'll call Callie's house," Frank said. He went to the phone. When he came back, he just shook his head.

For the next hour the boys all sat quietly, watching television. None of them really noticed what was on the screen. They just waited to see if Callie and Iola would show up at the restaurant.

At nearly ten o'clock, Chet broke the silence.

"I'm getting worried, guys," he said.

"We all are," Frank said.

"I'll go call Iola," Joe said.

"Let's drive over there," Chet suggested. "No reason to spook my folks if there isn't something to worry about."

Tony got up and began to clear the table. "Why don't you guys check to see if they left any messages. I'll clean up here."

"Do you want some help?" Joe asked.

"I got it," Tony said. "Just give me a call at home later to let me know the girls are okay."

Frank, Chet, and Joe left the pizza place. The three friends got in the van, each with a worried expression on his face.

"Let's drive over to Chet's house," Frank said. He got in the driver's seat. After everyone buckled his seat belt Frank put the car in gear. The silent drive to Chet's house seemed to take forever.

It was ten-thirty when the van pulled up in front of the Morton home.

"Callie's car isn't here," Frank said.

They walked up to the front door. Chet got out his key, but the door was unlocked.

When they entered the house, they saw that the light in the living room was lit.

"Iola?" Chet called as they headed toward the light.

"You mean she's not with you?" answered Chet's father as the boys entered the room. Mr. Morton, a large man who looked like an older version of his son, sat on a couch with his wife, a dead ringer for her daughter.

"Nope," Chet shook his head.

A worried look crossed Mrs. Morton's face. "Then where can she be?"

3 Girls in Trouble

Mrs. Morton's words hung in the air. Joe Hardy looked around the room. Everywhere he turned, he stared into a worried face.

"It certainly isn't like Iola to go off without telling somebody where she's going," Mr. Morton said.

"She was supposed to meet us at Pizza Palace after the television show," Frank said.

"Did something happen to change those plans?" Mr. Morton asked.

"Well, Sis and Callie did end up being guests on the show," Chet said. "Maybe they're hanging out with some of the people from *Monty Mania.*"

Chet's parents both gave their son quizzical looks. Chet began to fill them in on the details, drawing on the story that Frank and Joe had related to him earlier that evening.

Meanwhile, Frank had gone into the kitchen to use the phone. First he called his own house to see if the missing girls had left any word there. Then, after that phone call came up empty, he tried Callie's house. Nobody answered.

"Nobody's home at the Shaws'," Frank said when he returned to the living room.

Just then they heard a key in the front door. Everyone raced to the entryway.

"Iola!" Mr. Morton shouted as his daughter entered the house. "Are you all right?" Mrs. Morton gave her daughter a hug.

"Where have you been?" she asked.

Iola seemed taken aback by all of the attention. "Oh, just around."

"Where did you and Callie go after *Monty Mania?*" Frank asked. "Where's Callie?"

"She dropped me off and headed for home," Iola answered.

"Why didn't you meet us at the pizza place?" Joe asked. He crowded past Chet to put a reassuring hand on Iola's shoulder.

"Uh, no reason," Iola replied.

"Were you angry for what happened at the taping?" Joe asked.

"Or embarrassed?" Chet added.

"Not really," Iola responded. "Well, a little embarrassed, I guess."

"So what happened?"

"Well, Callie and I went backstage to sign the papers. Then Monty came back to talk to us. And then Callie and I just decided to go to the park."

"The park?" Joe sounded incredulous.

"Yeah, it's the weirdest thing. Callie and I got in the car, and we just sort of realized, 'Hey, we never spend any time together, just the two of us.' So we went to the park to talk."

"What did you talk about?" Chet asked.

"Oh, it's probably private," Mrs. Morton interjected. "Okay, everyone, it's late. Off to bed."

Joe gave Iola a hug. "I hope everything is okay. Call me if you want to talk."

"I'm fine, Joe." Iola briefly put her arms around Joe's back and gave him a squeeze.

Frank and Joe said good night to the Mortons, went out to the van, and headed for home.

The next morning Frank and Joe met with Chet in front of Bayport High School a half-hour before classes were to start. It gave the brothers a chance to fill in Chet on whatever case they might currently be working. Chet often proved a valuable asset to an investigation, acting as a sounding board for ideas and sometimes providing a little extra muscle if it was needed.

"Where's Iola?" Joe asked after he said good morning to Chet.

"She's with Callie," Chet responded. "Callie

picked up Iola real early, but I haven't seen them yet."

"Strange," Frank said. "Callie and Iola have always been friendly. They've been out with us on enough double dates to spend a lot of time together. But I wouldn't call them close. Not until the last sixteen or so hours."

Just as Frank finished his observation, Tony Prito arrived on his bicycle.

"Hey, gang," he said. He gave Joe a friendly pat on the shoulder. "How'd things wrap up last night?"

"Oh, man," Joe said sheepishly, "I was supposed to call you with an update. I'm so sorry. I hope you didn't sit around worried."

"Well, I was a little worried, but I managed to sleep." Everybody laughed. "So what happened? When did the girls show up?"

"It was around eleven," Chet said. "Iola and Callie just hung out with each other all evening."

"That's it?" Tony asked. "That's the great mystery?"

Before anybody could add anything to the conversation, Frank's attention was drawn to the school parking lot.

"Hey, there are Callie and Iola now," he said, pointing to Callie's car as it pulled into a parking space. The four boys began to walk over to the car. Tony waved to the girls and then veered off toward the bike rack to lock up his ten-speed.

"Good morning, you two," Frank said. The group of friends stood in the parking lot in silence for a moment.

"So, are you two completely avoiding us since yesterday?" Joe asked.

Iola leaned against Joe. "Oh, don't be silly, Joe. What could possibly be wrong?"

"Well, you have been a little mysterious since the television taping yesterday," Frank said. He gave a worried glance to Callie. "Are you guys mad at us?"

Callie reached out and took Frank's hand. "Nothing is the matter," she said. "Iola and I just realized after our starring performance yesterday, that we really know each other only through you and Joe."

"And me," Chet interjected. His face was animated, trying to break a little of the tension with humor.

"And Chet," Callie added. "Anyway, we took the opportunity to spend some time alone to see if there was more of a connection between us than just the Brothers Hardy."

"And?" Joe asked.

"And we found out—" Iola began to say. But a loud blaring of car horns and the call of a booming voice crackling through a bullhorn drowned out her words.

"Bayport's ballplayers are bums!" shouted the disembodied voice. Joe craned his neck, scanning the parking lot to see where the ruckus was coming from. He spotted a large red classic convertible car slowly wending its way through the rows of parked cars.

"Who are the rich kids?" Joe began to say, but again his words were drowned out by the blaring car horn.

"Shoreham is gonna show Bayport who's boss!"

The speeding car made its way into the row where the group of friends stood. They could all read a large sign that was being waved in the air by one of the car's occupants.

"Shoreham baseball rules," Frank read aloud.

"The nerve of those guys!" Chet said. "Coming to our turf before the season's even started."

The convertible drove closer to where everybody was standing. As it approached the group, it began to accelerate.

"Whooh! Yeah!" shouted a boy as the car sped past. He raised both arms and hurled two large, round, wobbly projectiles. The missiles careened through the air, straight at Joe and Callie. Before either of them could move, they were hit, leaving them soaking wet as the Shoreham students sped out of the parking lot.

"Why those . . ." Joe growled through gritted teeth.

"Water balloons!" Callie shouted at the same time. "I'm soaked, and so are my books!"

Frank reached into his gym bag and took out a

fresh towel and handed it to Callie. Joe just stood there dripping.

"I guess I'll have to get a towel from my locker," he said. The group began to walk toward the front entrance of the school.

Just then a police car pulled into the parking lot. It rolled to a stop at the foot of the steps. Con Riley, a senior officer with the Bayport police force, got out of the passenger side. The driver of the car, a uniformed police officer whom nobody recognized, stayed in the vehicle.

"Con!" Frank called out to the man who had helped the Hardys break several cases. "Are you here chasing those punks from Shoreham?" he asked as everyone converged on the police car. "You just missed them."

A quizzical look crossed the man's face. "What are you talking about?"

"Those guys from Shoreham High who just came racing through our parking lot, hurling water balloons," Joe said. He pointed in the direction in which the red car had driven off.

"I have no idea what you're babbling about, Joe," Con said. "But I sure wish something like that was what brought me here."

"Why *are* you here?" Frank asked. He cocked his head toward the patrol car.

"I came as a favor to you and your brother."

"Oh, no—has something happened to Dad?" Joe asked, a worried look crossing his wet face. The boys' father, Fenton Hardy, had been a New York City police officer, but years ago he had gone into private practice as a detective.

"Thankfully, no," Con answered.

"So, what's the favor?" Joe asked.

"I thought it would smooth things if I was the one to do it, seeing as we're all friends."

"Con, you're scaring me," Frank said. "Do what?"

Con pointed a finger.

"Iola Morton and Callie Shaw," he said, "you are hereby placed under arrest."

4 Clueless at the Police Station

"What do you mean 'under arrest'?" Chet shouted with shock.

The uniformed Officer got out of the patrol car.

"I'll handle this," Con said, calling over his shoulder. Then he looked at the group of friends. "Just what I said. I have to arrest them."

"Cuffs, sir?" the uniformed officer, apparently a rookie, asked.

"Not for these kids," Con answered.

"But procedure?"

"Won't be necessary, Officer," Con said through gritted teeth.

"What is happening here?" Joe asked.

Con ignored the question. Instead he turned to Callie and Iola.

"You have the right to remain silent," he began.

"Frank," Callie said. Confusion crossed both girls' faces.

"Just do what he says," Frank replied.

Con began to read the girls their Miranda Rights once more. When he had finished and they had responded that they understood them, Con turned to the other cop. The officer opened the back door of the police cruiser and motioned the girls inside with a cock of his head.

"What are they being arrested for?" Joe asked.

"I can't tell you," Con replied.

"Hey, you can't just cart off my sister without telling us why!" Chet looked as if he was going to lose complete control of his temper.

"What do you mean you can't tell us?" Frank said. "You can't arrest somebody without telling them why."

"I'll tell them once we drive away," Con said.

"Why are you deliberately keeping the crime from the rest of us?" Chet asked. "That's my sister you're taking to jail."

Con looked pained. "I don't like being this way," he said. "Especially with you guys. But I have my orders."

Con walked around the car and opened the passenger door. "I'm sorry," he said as he got into the car.

After the police drove off with Callie and Iola, Tony Prito came jogging up to the group of dumb-struck boys.

"What was that all about?" he asked.

"I don't know," Joe said angrily. "But I plan to find out."

"I'd better call my parents before we head off to the police station," Chet said.

"Going to the precinct house is a good idea," Frank said. "But I think Joe and I should go alone."

"No way!" Chet was steamed. "They might be your girlfriends, but Iola is my sister."

"I don't like the way this smells," Frank said. "Con said he's under orders not to let us in on what's going on, but Joe and I are regular visitors to the police station. We might be able to get more information if just the two of us go in there. A more personal approach might get them to loosen up a little."

"My brother is right." Joe put a reassuring hand on Chet's shoulder. "If we all go in there, they might clam up. Let us see what we can dig up."

"Uh, what about school?" Tony asked sheepishly.

"You two go call Chet's folks and Callie's parents. Then cover for us in class. We'll contact you as soon as we know something."

"I'm not too happy about this," Chet said. "But I guess you guys are right. Just don't let anything happen to my sister or Callie."

"Never have," Joe said as he began to walk toward his van.

"And never will," added Frank.

When Frank and Joe arrived at the police station, they headed straight for the second floor. They figured that Con would try to get the girls through booking as quickly as possible; except for not cuffing the girls, he seemed quite preoccupied with procedure in this case. Their instincts proved correct; Callie and Iola were halfway through the fingerprinting process just as Frank and Joe ascended the stairs.

"Joe! Frank!" Iola shouted when she spotted the brothers. Joe and Frank headed straight for the girls.

"Are you two all right?" Frank asked.

"Just peachy," Callie said, rolling her eyes.

Joe looked all around, surveying the situation. He saw Con at his desk as the girls were being ushered through the process by a uniformed female officer they had never met before. The woman did not seem interested in the presence of the Hardys; she appeared to want to get the booking process and paperwork finished.

"What did they arrest you for?" Joe asked.

"Con said it was for—" Callie began to say. However, before she could finish her sentence, a stern "Enough" that was shouted from across the room cut off her words. The four teens looked across the room and spotted Police Chief Collig. The Bayport police commander stormed across the room. Con, hearing the commotion, came hurrying after him.

"You two are prohibited from speaking to anybody but your parents and lawyers," Collig said with a wag of his finger. He motioned to the officer with his head. "Split them up," he said crisply. "Interrogation Two and Five." The officer immediately ushered Iola and Callie away.

"What was that—what is this—all about?" Frank asked.

"This is about you two interfering with an investigation," Collig replied.

"An investigation of what?" Joe asked with anger.

"Let it go for now," Con said.

"I don't want these two anywhere near this case," Collig said to Con. "Am I clear?"

"Crystal," Con replied curtly.

Just then Chief Collig's assistant called to him from across the room. "Chief," he said, holding up a phone receiver, "it's the mayor again." Collig let out a heavy breath, turned and went to his office.

"Come on, Con," Frank said when the chief was out of earshot. "What gives?"

"Collig is serious about this, guys," Con said. "More so than usual. He doesn't want you two near this case."

"What case?" Joe asked.

"Uh-uh, you won't find out from me."

Joe and Frank both gave Con a pleading look.

"All I can do for you is promise to keep an eye on your friends," Con said. "It'll have to be enough for now."

"For now," Joe said curtly.

"Thanks, Con," Frank added, a bit more smoothly.

"I have to go check on them." Con turned to head off toward where Callie and Iola had been led moments before.

Frank and Joe looked at each other and shook their heads.

"You watch?" Joe asked.

Frank nodded his head. "You snoop around for some clues."

The brothers, who were frequent visitors to the Bayport Police Station, nonchalantly walked across the room to Con Riley's desk. Nobody looked up from what they were doing to question their presence there.

Joe leaned back against Con's desk, while Frank stationed himself a few feet away, his eyes glued to the hallway where the interrogation rooms were located. Joe yawned, stretched, and leaned back. On the desk were stacks of folders, a coffee cup, pencils, pens, and other clutter.

Con's not usually this messy, Joe thought. From where Joe was standing he was unable to see fully the file folders and papers that were at the center of the desk.

That's probably what I want to read, Joe thought. It's what he's currently working on.

Joe moved his body along the desk, using one hip to shift a stack of files a bit to give him a clearer view of the papers he wanted a better look at. He spotted an arrest warrant sitting on top of a file folder. He couldn't make out what it said, though.

Joe stretched and yawned once more, and as he moved his arms behind his back, he swiped the folder and warrant to the floor. They landed on the opposite side of the desk from where he was standing.

"Clumsy me," he said to nobody in particular. Joe circled the desk and moved the chair out of the way so he could get to the papers. The arrest warrant, he could now read, was for Callie Shaw and Iola Morton. Joe scanned the legal mumbo jumbo, looking for the reason the warrant was issued. His eyes went wide.

"Robbery?" he mumbled.

Joe was so perplexed by what he just read that he failed to hear his brother coughing.

"Joe" came a harsh whisper two seconds later, followed by what sounded like Frank going into a huge coughing fit. That caught the younger Hardy's attention. He immediately began to scoop up the papers and folder he had pushed off the desk. As he began to stand up he chanced a quick glance at the top page inside the file. Again his eyes went wide with confusion.

"Just what do you think you're doing?" came a sudden loud and very disappointed-sounding voice.

5 Answering Some Questions

Joe smiled as he put the file folder back on top of the desk. He straightened the papers, moved the coffee mug, and lined up some pencils.

"Uh, just helping you clean up some of this mess," he said sheepishly, staring straight into the eyes of Con Riley.

Then he added with more confidence, "You just seem so busy and all, and I know how much you like a neat desk." Joe walked around the desk to stand next to his brother. There was an awkward silence as Con just shook his head.

"I trusted you boys," Con said sadly. "I told you to stay out of this."

"Come on, Con," Frank said. "We're the same guys you always have trusted and always can trust. But you can't expect us to sit on the sidelines when our girlfriends have just been arrested for who knows what."

Joe cleared his throat. At this point the only person standing there who didn't know why the girls had been arrested was Frank. Joe wanted to tell his brother what he had read, but he knew it was best not to let Con know what he had read inside the file folder.

"Anyway," Con said, "I'm glad you're both still here. Saves me the trouble of having to round you up."

"Round us up?" Frank asked. "Why, are you arresting us also?"

"No," Con said with a shake of his head. "But the chief does want to ask you some questions."

"About what?" Frank asked. Con pursed his lips and shook his head without saying a word.

"Before we settle down for a chat with the chief," Joe said, "I need to use the bathroom."

"Whatever," Con replied.

Joe stepped past his brother. As he did so, he lightly elbowed Frank in the ribs.

"Oh," Frank said. "I have to go, too."

Con smirked at the brothers.

"Big breakfast," Frank said, patting his stomach.

"Uh-huh," Con said nodding his head. "Big breakfast. Sure, go ahead. Be quick and then meet me in Interrogation One."

Frank and Joe headed for the bathroom. Once

they were inside, Joe held a finger to his lips, keeping Frank silent for a moment. He motioned to the stalls. The brothers swiftly peeked under each stall door to make sure nobody else was in the room. Satisfied that they were alone, Joe began to whisper.

"Do you think he suspected that we wanted to talk?" he said, knowing full well that they hadn't put anything over on Officer Riley.

Frank chuckled. "So what did you find out?"

"Two things, maybe related, maybe not. First, the girls were arrested for robbery."

"Robbery," Frank said, his voice rising above a whisper. Just then the door opened and a detective entered the bathroom. Joe remembered his name as Mike Dreher, a hard-nosed veteran who worked homicide cases.

"Boys," the detective said as he went into a stall.

"Detective Dreher," Joe said. Then he led Frank over to the row of sinks and turned on the water in two of them. He washed his hands, and Frank followed suit.

"What else?" Frank asked.

"Con's working the Jewelry Exchange case."

"What does that have to do with the girls? The cops don't think Callie and Iola are involved with that, do they?"

Joe just shrugged his shoulders. The toilet flushed and Detective Dreher approached the sinks. Frank and Joe dried their hands in silence and left the bathroom. They went to Interrogation Room One, where Con Riley was waiting for them.

"Have a seat, boys." Con motioned to some chairs arrayed around an old wooden table. Frank and Joe both sat down. Con closed the door to the room partway.

"I am required to inform you that you are about to be officially questioned," he said curtly.

"Why all the formality, Con?" Frank asked.

Con did not reply to the question. Instead he said, "Do you understand?"

"Sure," Joe said. "If that's the way it's going to be. Should we have a lawyer present?"

"You have that right," Con replied.

"But why waste time?" Chief Collig came barging into the interrogation room. He slammed the door shut behind him. "Unless you have something to hide?"

"What's to hide?" Joe asked angrily. "We're not the ones who arrested two girls and refuse to tell anybody why."

"That's enough, Joe," Frank said.

"You should listen to your brother," Collig said. "He must have got all the brains in the family."

"Chief, that was uncalled for," Con said. "Look, boys, I can tell you that what we want to know may help your friends."

"Or it may hurt them," Joe said.

"Get this, Hardy," the chief said. He pulled up

a chair, turned it around, and sat down facing the Hardys. He leaned in close to Joe. "Easy way or hard way? Answer the questions—easy. Hard is what we call obstructing justice."

Joe stared directly into Collig's eyes. The chief had never made it a secret that he didn't like the brother detectives; he had always found them obtrusive and was perhaps sometimes embarrassed that they had solved cases that the Bayport Police Department had had trouble bringing to a close. But Joe didn't appreciate his belligerent approach and wasn't about to back down when the fate of his friends was at stake.

"Easy way," Frank finally said, breaking the tension. "We're trusting you here, Con. Plus, we have nothing to hide."

Chief Collig made a clucking sound and shook his head. He scooted his chair back a few inches from Joe.

"Good idea," Con said. "Okay, we know you two are pretty close with Ms. Shaw and Ms. Morton. Do you have any knowledge of their whereabouts yesterday?"

Joe crossed his arms and just sat silently. After a moment Frank said, "They were at school. Had lunch with them as a matter of fact."

"What about after school?" Collig asked meanly.

"Chief Collig," Joe said, "the bad cop act is wearing thin."

"Who said I was acting?"

"Excuse me," Joe replied. "Overacting."

"What my brother is trying to say is, we agree to cooperate, so how about everybody just playing nice."

"Good idea, Frank," Con said. "Anyway, back to the question: Do you know anything about their whereabouts after school?"

"They were with us at the Bayport Television Studio for a taping of the *Monty Mania* show."

"I love that show," Con said. "Did he hypnotize anybody?"

"As a matter of fact—" Frank began.

"Enough with the TV show already!" Collig boomed. "We know that show doesn't start taping until four o'clock. Were the two girls with you from after school until the show started?"

The Hardy brothers both hesitated.

"That answers that question," Collig said.

"Okay," Joe said. "No they weren't. They met us there at three forty-five."

"Do you know where they were from the end of school—what is that, two-thirty?—until three forty-five?"

"They both wanted to change their clothes," Frank said.

"That's all you know?" Collig asked.

"That's all we know about after school until they met us," Frank said.

"What time did the show end?" Con asked.

"Taping ended around six-forty," Frank said.

"And what happened after that?"

"We went to the Pizza Palace," Joe said. He knew what question was coming next, but he was hoping it wouldn't get asked. "We had some dinner," he added, trying to delay the inevitable.

"Did the ladies go with you?" Con asked.

"No," Frank said softly. "No, they didn't."

Chief Collig stood up and pushed his chair back under the table.

"Hmmm. Interesting," he said. "Now the million-dollar question: When did you next see them?"

Joe let out a long breath. He glanced around the room. Frank looked at his own shoes.

"Need that one read back to you?" Collig chided.

"We saw Iola around eleven at her house," Frank said. "Callie we didn't see until the next morning at school just before they were arrested."

There was silence in the room for several heartbeats.

"Can we go now?"

"Sure, Joe, you can go," Con said.

Frank and Joe got up from the table and headed for the door of the interrogation room.

"Oh, one more thing," Collig said. "Any witnesses to where you two were after the show?"

"Chet Morton and Tony Prito and about half a dozen other people who came into the pizza place," Joe said. He didn't want to use his friends' names, but he knew it was inevitable.

"A whole gang of teens," Collig sneered.

"What was that?" Joe asked, perturbed at Collig's choice of words. Joe stepped away from the door and moved into the center of the room. The muscular teen leaned his hands against the table. He stared into Ezra Collig's weathered eyes.

"Teens, friends, they hang together, cover for one another."

"Well, if we're covering for Callie and Iola," Joe said, "we did a pretty bad job of it."

"Yeah, pretty bad," Collig said. Just then Con put his hand on his commander's shoulder, almost as if it was a choreographed stage move. The two police officers walked to the far side of the room. They spoke in hushed tones for a couple of minutes.

Joe gave Frank a quizzical look. Frank shrugged his shoulders and walked over to stand next to Joe.

When the two men turned their attention back to the brothers, Joe asked, "So, what else do you want to know? What we had for dinner? If Tony got us a discount? What?"

"Hey, you get a discount?" Con asked. Some of the tension went out of the room. "So," Con continued, "how's it look for Bayport's baseball team this season?"

"Pretty good," Frank answered.

"Shoreham's not going to give you any trouble?"

Con asked. "Especially with Rojas and Wingfoot gone."

"Okay, Riley," Collig cut in. "That's enough. I know you're chummy with these kids, but I want them away from this case. Or *you're* going to be away from it. Clear?"

"Sorry, sir," Con said.

Collig turned to Frank and Joe. "I don't want to see you boys around here."

"What about Iola and Callie?" Joe asked.

"I'll repeat, I do not want to hear, sniff, or see that you two are meddling with this case."

"What case?" Frank asked. "You still haven't told us what's going on with our friends."

Collig did not reply. His eyes narrowed as he looked at something that had caught his attention. He stepped past Frank and Joe, walking briskly to the blinds that covered the interrogation room's window, a window that looked out onto the station's central area.

He poked at the blinds with his fingers. "What is going on out there?" He exhaled with disbelief.

Frank and Joe could hear shouts of anger coming from the other side of the window. Then they heard the distinct clatter of furniture being overturned.

"Oh, man," Chief Collig murmured through gritted teeth. "Not in a room full of cops."

6 Putting the Pieces Together

Chief Collig threw open the door and bolted into the central office. Frank, Joe, and Con Riley could all hear a loud commotion emanating from the main room. Frank and Joe were through the door right on Collig's heels, with Riley two steps behind them.

"What's going on out here?" Collig growled. It was hard to hear him over the noise. Most of the police officers were standing at their desks, frozen, while a few ran toward what looked like a wrestling match at the top of the stairs. It appeared that several officers were trying to control a large man, but neither Frank nor Joe could make out who it was through the twist of bodies.

Collig raced across the room.

"Hold it!" he shouted. "Hold it!"

As Collig got closer, the melee calmed down a bit. However, the chief still blocked Frank and Joe's view of who was being detained. From where they stood, it appeared that three officers were holding back one very enraged man.

"I just want to see my daughter!" the man yelled.

Frank immediately recognized the voice of a man he had spent a lot of time talking to over the last couple of years.

"Mr. Shaw?" Frank trotted over to the group of men.

"Mr. Who? Oh, no." Collig put his right hand on one officer's shoulder and his left on another's. "Okay. It's okay, boys. Calm down. Let him go." The cops who were holding the man eased their grip. After a moment's hesitation they let go and stepped back a few paces.

"Mr. Shaw?" Frank asked as he maneuvered himself next to the angered man. "What happened?"

Joe trotted up. "Police brutality?" he asked sarcastically. "Or maybe they won't let him talk to Callie either."

"That's exactly it!" Mr. Shaw shouted. "They won't let me see my daughter!"

"Look, sir," Collig said. "I am so sorry."

"You should be," Mr. Shaw growled. "I hear my little girl is arrested, and I come down here to see her, but your goon squad won't tell me anything."

"Again, I apologize. They're under strict orders that the girls have no visitors." Collig turned his head to shout at the squad room. "But I didn't mean their parents." He put an arm around Mr. Shaw's shoulder.

"Here," he said. "Let me personally take you down to see your daughter."

Chief Collig ushered Mr. Shaw down the stairs before Frank or Joe could get in a word.

"Looks like he doesn't know what's going on either," Frank said.

"Well, they'll have to tell him," Joe said. The two brothers began to trot down the stairs. They spotted the chief and Mr. Shaw just as they rounded a corner, heading deeper into the precinct house toward the holding cells.

"Should we try to tag along?" Joe asked.

"Nah. Collig won't let us get close. We might as well head back to school. We'll give Callie's dad a call later and see what he might have learned."

The brothers headed out to their van. In silence they got in, Frank taking the driver's seat, and began the journey back to school.

"We pretty much missed morning classes," Joe said, making idle conversation.

"I hope Chet and Tony took good notes for us," Frank said. "I was looking forward to being a student again for a while. No cases, just classes."

"And baseball practice," Joe said. "For once I'd like to make it through a season without missing practice. I don't want any excuses, win or lose, this year."

"We'll beat Shoreham, bro. We've got a dynamite team this year."

"So do they, unless Rojas and Wingfoot go to jail. Without them, they'll have an excuse if they lose."

Frank's eyes lit up. He sat higher in the driver's seat and snapped his fingers once.

"What class did you miss?" he asked happily.

"Math. Why?"

"Well, you get an A! You just helped with some stellar addition and problem solving."

"You're losing me here, Frank."

"Baseball season! That's the key."

"Okay, baseball. Got ya. Baseball is going to get Iola and Callie cleared of robbery."

"It might," Frank said. "Remember when Con asked us about our chances against Shoreham?"

"Yeah. Small talk. Con's great at small talk."

"And at giving us clues. He knows you saw what was in that file, or at least he figures you might have seen something. He wanted us to know that what is happening with the girls really is connected to the robbery at the Jewelry Exchange."

"And?"

"So he's given us a place to start. Find out what happened at the Jewelry Exchange and we can clear the girls."

"In fact," Joe said, catching on to Con's clue,

"he gave us two places to start. He wanted us to be concerned specifically with Rojas and Wingfoot. Maybe he figures we can get to them in a way that the cops can't."

Frank slowed down as he made a left turn into Bayport High's parking lot. "So we have two places to check, the Jewelry Exchange and the alleged thieves," he said.

"Great"—Joe laughed—"now even the police are giving us homework."

"I wonder if we can get extra credit," Frank said as he pulled the van into a parking space. He cut the engine and hopped out, grabbing his books from the backseat. The brothers headed into the main building just as the bell rang.

"Well, we made it back in time for lunch. We're sure to ace that class," Joe said. "Let's find Chet and Tony and fill them in on what happened at the police station."

Frank and Joe made their way to the cafeteria. When they entered the large room, it was already teeming with a mass of students. Joe craned his head, surveying the crowd. He spotted Chet and Tony sitting at a table by the window. The two were alone, sitting in silence, picking at their food. Even Chet's legendary appetite had deserted him.

"Frank and Joe Hardy to Long Face Central," Joe said as he approached the table. He sat down next to Chet.

"Not much to celebrate," Chet said.

Frank sat on the bench next to Tony. "Not right now," he said. "But we're working on it."

"So you got some information from the cops?"

"If you call getting threatened with obstruction of justice information," Joe said.

"Joe's understating our success," Frank quickly added.

"So what did you find out? Did you see my sister? What did they say?"

"In order," Frank said. "Little, but it may be important. Yes. And not much before Chief Collig cut them off."

"Details," Tony said. "We had English literature this morning, so you can use long sentences."

Some tension left the table with Tony's comment. After some chuckles, the group huddled closer together.

"Callie and Iola were arrested for robbery," Frank revealed in a low voice.

"My sister?" Chet yelled. Joe held up a silencing finger, indicating that he preferred the whole school not be let in on the facts.

"R-robbery?" Chet stammered in a quieter voice. "What did they steal?"

"Allegedly steal." Tony corrected his frenetic friend.

"We're not certain," Joe said, "but we think they're suspects in the Jewelry Exchange heist."

"Like the girls are into jewelry?" Tony sounded

incredulous. "I mean, they are girls and all, but flashy gold and sparkling diamonds are not their speed."

"That's for sure," Frank agreed. "When I gave Callie a charm bracelet for her birthday, she said she was afraid to wear such a nice piece of jewelry."

"Anyway," Chet said, "I thought the cops had collared Rojas and Wingfoot from Shoreham High for that job."

"Maybe they think that those two robbed the store to get the jewels to give the girls," Tony said.

"I don't think they even know Callie and Iola, let alone know them well enough to steal a million dollars in baubles for them," Joe said. "And anyway, if that was the case, the cops would have just brought the girls in for questioning."

"Still, we do plan to follow up the Rojas and Wingfoot angle," Frank added.

"All of this speculation is giving me a headache," Chet said. He looked at his watch. "I've got time to call my parents to see what they found out at the station. Maybe they have some clearer information."

Chet got up from the table and left the cafeteria. The three other friends sat in silence, picking at their lunches for the five minutes that he was gone. When he returned, Chet wore a worried frown on his face.

"Didn't hit a home run, I take it," Joe said.

Chet shook his head. "Didn't even get to swing the bat."

"They didn't tell you anything about your own sister being arrested?" Tony was amazed.

"They said the police told them that they could reveal nothing, not even to me. Specifically to me, in fact."

"They must have your mom and dad pretty shaken up to be able to get them to go for such a gag order."

"You got that straight, Frank. My mom sounded very nervous. Then my dad got on the phone and grilled me about last night."

"How so?" Joe asked.

"Where I was, who I was with. Times, travel routes, the whole nine yards. It was like he was investigating me."

"Wow, talk about overreactions," Tony said.

"You might be next, buddy," Chet replied. "He asked for your mom's number."

"Just because we were all together last night? Well, the guys at the pizza place have us covered."

"The police grilled us about what we were up to last night also," Frank said.

Joe put his chin in his hand and leaned his elbow against the table. He furrowed his brow, deep in thought.

"Doing chemistry in your head again, Joe?"

"No, Frank, more addition. Remember when we were about to leave the interrogation room? When

Collig made that crack about teens hanging together?"

"Collig is always making cracks about us. I think he was born a crotchety middle-aged man. He's not fond of youth, which to him is anybody a day or more younger than he is."

"That's my point," Joe said. "He doesn't like teenagers. To him we're all one step away from making trouble. Emphasis this time on the word *all.*"

"I think I follow you now," Frank said.

"Want to let us in on it?" Chet asked.

"Gangs," Joe said. The word hung in the air.

After a moment Tony spoke. "And he thinks we're a gang?"

"Wouldn't be the first time," Frank said.

"So he thinks we're all part of some jewelry store–robbing gang? That's a little hard to swallow."

"Not for you, Chet," Joe said with a smile.

"Yeah, but a gang like that is big-time stuff," Tony said. "People get hurt, serious crimes are committed. Nothing like that happens here in Bayport."

"We've been fortunate," Frank replied. "And part of that may be because the police chief has strict views on young people. Maybe he has a fear, what with the Jewelry Exchange robbery, that gangs are making a debut in Bayport."

"That still doesn't tie us or Iola and Callie into it at all," Chet said.

"Not yet," Joe responded. "But we're going to work on that angle later this afternoon."

"Work on it how?" Tony asked.

"Frank and I are going shopping in the jewelry district."

"After we catch some classes," Frank added.

After school Frank and Joe met at the van.

"Man, believe it or not, it was nice to be a student for a little while," Frank said.

Joe climbed into the van. "I hear you," he said with a nod. "History class almost took my mind off our girlfriends' being in jail."

"They'll be out soon," Frank said. "Robbery doesn't require them to be held without bail. I figure they'll be out by dinnertime."

The rest of the drive to the Jewelry Exchange was filled with talk of classwork and studying. The brothers even quizzed each other to stay mentally sharp. It was an invigorating exercise that helped keep their minds ready for whatever might come their way, on or off a case.

"Ah, here we are," Frank said as he pulled into the store's parking lot.

"I hope we're not underdressed," Joe said as he looked at some of the people going in and out of the store's front door. Everybody he saw was wearing either a suit or a fashionable dress.

"Or underage," Frank added.

Once the two were inside the Jewelry Exchange, all three of the shop's workers and most of its dozen or so customers turned a disapproving eye toward the Hardys.

"Maybe the thief hit this place because he doesn't like snooty people," Joe whispered.

"Just try to be casual," Frank replied. "We're here looking for a present for Mom or something."

The two brothers split up, Frank moving toward the standing glass cases on the left and Joe heading over to the counters on the right. Both noted the locks on the cases and cabinets; they were standard medium-security locks, most likely hardwired to an alarm system. Frank concentrated on getting the rhythm of the clientele, but all he could observe was that he and Joe were the only ones who looked out of place. However, the store was awfully busy, especially for having been robbed two nights earlier. It made Frank wonder how the stock could have been replenished so quickly.

Joe moved toward the back of the store, near where he could see a door that probably led to some back rooms. The door was partially opened, only revealing a desk and door to Joe, whose field of vision was limited. Joe glanced down at a case of gold necklaces, so as not to appear to be staring at the door. When he chanced another look, he saw somebody move inside the office. Joe could see only the person's pants leg, and he was sure that what he saw was not the standard slacks that someone would wear with a suit. The leg looked as if it belonged to work overalls.

"May I help you?" came a shrill voice from behind Joe.

"Uh, yeah," Joe replied. He turned around to peer into the face of a thin, pale man with wire-rimmed glasses and a disapproving stare. "I was hoping to get something nice for my mother."

"Well, that is certainly possible, depending on what price range you were considering."

"I was thinking," Joe began, but there was no way he could be heard over the sudden crash of glass and the wailing of the loudest alarm he had ever heard.

7 The Blind Eye

At the sound of the alarm, Joe immediately spun around to face the door. He glimpsed Frank out of the corner of his eye, but his vision was partially obscured by the half dozen or so patrons who were frantically heading for the exit. The first person to reach the exit slammed against the door with little result.

An auto-locking mechanism, Joe thought.

The alarm kept up its incessant wailing, so Joe knew the only way to communicate with his brother was to make his way over to him. He began to push past a couple of shoppers, when he saw that Frank was moving toward the door. Joe followed his brother's gaze and realized what he was looking at so intensely.

"Gun!" Joe cried as instinct took over in both of

the Hardys. They had spotted a well-dressed man who stood just to the left of the front door as he reached into his sports coat and drew out a silver handgun. Before the man could take aim at any target, both Frank and Joe were flying toward him.

Frank crouched low as he approached the man. At that same moment Joe, who was coming from the man's blind side, leaped forward through the air. Both brothers crashed into the man at the same instant, Frank wrapping his arm around the man's legs while Joe struck against his midsection. The man fell backward, landing in a heap with Frank and Joe entwined around him.

"The gun!" Frank yelled, and Joe heard him; the alarm had finally stopped ringing.

Joe reached up and pinned the man's arm to the ground. The guy was strong, but Joe had the advantage of surprise and leverage. The gun stayed in the man's hand, but he was unable to raise his arm to aim a shot.

"Get off me, you goofs!" The man flailed his legs, but Frank held them fast.

"Drop the gun!" Joe demanded.

"Oh, my!" screeched a voice from the middle of the store. "Do get off him!"

Neither Frank nor Joe loosened their grip. The three continued to struggle on the floor.

"I'm security!" the man with the gun shouted.

"Yeah, right," Frank said. "We'll just let the police sort this out."

Joe felt a hand on his shoulder. From the corner of his eye, he could see the salesman who had questioned him just before the alarm had sounded.

"He really is store security," the salesman said.

Frank and Joe looked at each other for a second. Then they loosened their grip. They cautiously got up off the man.

"Uh, sorry," Frank said, extending his hand. The man hesitated. Then he lifted the gun and pointed it at the brothers.

"Whoa," Joe exhaled. "We're the good guys."

"We thought you were robbing the store," Frank said.

"Robbing the store?" The salesman guffawed. "Mr. Friedman is here to provide security."

Joe looked at the salesman. It was then that he noticed that there was a name tag pinned to his jacket: Jack Jones—Manager.

Mr. Friedman lowered the gun. He reached into the pocket of his now very wrinkled sports coat.

"Here," he said gruffly. He handed a laminated ID badge to Frank. On it was his picture along with a company logo.

"Eye Spy Security?" Frank read. He handed back the badge.

"Yeah," Mr. Friedman replied, getting to his feet. "We provide the security system here."

"Which seems to be back in working order," Mr. Jones said.

"Why did the alarm sound?" Friedman asked. "Did someone smash a case?"

"Nah," came a voice from the back of the room. "Wiring overheated," said a man in dark coveralls. The logo on his work clothes identified him as part of Eye Spy Security, too. "When it sparked, I dropped my drill, and it smashed through one of the cases I was wiring in back, setting off the screamer. I need some new pieces from the truck."

The workman walked toward the front of the store. He keyed a code into the keypad on the wall next to the entrance. There was a click, and he pushed open the door.

"Uh," said a middle-aged woman raising her hand, "can we leave now?"

"Are all cases still closed and locked?" Mr. Friedman asked the store manager. Mr. Jones gave a questioning look toward the three other workers in the store. They all nodded.

"Sure, you can go."

Every patron of the Jewelry Exchange immediately exited the shop. In less than one minute the only people left in the store were Frank and Joe, Mr. Friedman, and the store staff.

"Great," Frank said quietly to Joe. "We netted zero information."

Joe looked at the front door. "We're not through here yet."

"You have a plan?"

"I'm going to smooth-talk the manager to see what I can find out."

"What should I do?"

"Help this guy with all those boxes." Joe pointed through the front door as he backed away from his brother. Outside the door, the installation man from Eye Spy Security struggled to enter the store without dropping any of the several boxes he was carrying.

"Here," Frank said as he pulled open the door, "let me get that for you."

"Thanks, buddy." The man balanced a large box against his shoulder.

"Let me take the smaller boxes," Frank said as he took a few of the parcels from the man. Before the man could object or accept, Frank was already heading toward the backroom.

"I'll put these back here," he said.

"Thanks," the Eye Spy man replied as he followed Frank.

When Frank entered the backroom, he spotted a desk with a computer on it, a filing cabinet, and several chairs. Off to his left was another door.

"Just through there," said the workman with a flick of his head.

"No problem," Frank said. He headed through the interior door, which led him to another room, much larger than the office. In it was a long table against the side wall. On the table were a few open boxes, a worn-out toolbox, and some stray wires. Next to the table was a ladder. Frank put the boxes on the table. As he passed the ladder, he looked up at the ceiling. A few panels were pushed open, revealing wires and electrical sockets.

The workman put the large box on the table and climbed the ladder.

"So," Frank started, "a lot of excitement for one day—uh, what did you say your name was?"

"Bill," the worker replied as he stuck his head through an open ceiling panel.

"I'm Frank. So, it must be a pretty sophisticated security system here, Bill."

"Hand me that flathead screwdriver?" Without removing his head from the hole, Bill reached down toward Frank. "The one we're installing now is a top-notch system all right. The store should have gone with it in the first place."

"Who provided the first system?" Frank handed Bill the screwdriver.

"We did," Bill replied, indicating Eye Spy Security. "But to cut costs, the store went with an older model. Sure, it had cameras, alarms, and sensors—the whole nine yards. But the electronics weren't the greatest. That's why the cameras malfunctioned the other night."

"Really?"

"Yeah, all but one of them. The one that caught those two kids robbing the place."

"How did they even get in here?"

Bill ducked his head out and handed Frank the screwdriver.

"Some number two blue cable."

"They used what?" Frank asked. "What's number two blue cable?"

"I need some," Bill said, pointing his finger. "It's in that box over there."

Frank turned to the table and retrieved the wire the workman had asked for.

"Anyway," Bill continued once his head was back up in the ceiling, "from the way most of these wires were cooked, I figure they must have sent a huge electrical pulse through the whole system."

"How'd two kids figure out how to do that?"

"Who knows? These days, they probably found the instructions posted somewhere on the Internet. Anyway, they were so confident of their handiwork with the security system they didn't even wear masks when they pulled the heist."

Bill made a grunting sound. "There," he said as he descended the ladder. "Ready for the new cameras. Hey, thanks for the hand, Frank," Bill said, patting Frank on the shoulder.

Frank went back into the store and found Joe.

"Learn anything?" Frank asked as they went out to the van.

"Bits and pieces. Eye Spy Security agreed to replace the security system for free. If the jewels aren't recovered, insurance will cover the cost."

"So we could be looking at some sort of insurance scam," Frank said. "Maybe the robbery was a cover. Steal the jewels, sell them elsewhere, and claim the insurance money."

Joe started up the van. "But how does that involve Rojas and Wingfoot?"

"The store's owner could have brought them in as fall guys. Promise them some fast, easy cash, have them rob the place, and then double-cross them so they take the rap for it."

"Guess that points us to our next stop," Joe said. "Let's chat with the suspects. Shoreham started baseball practice today, so Rojas and Wingfoot should be at the school."

While they drove to Shoreham High School, Frank filled in his brother on what he had learned at the store. Joe was intrigued by Bill's comment about the thieves not wearing any masks.

"From the few times we played against Rojas and Wingfoot, I'd definitely take them as the confident type. But to have the know-how to short out an alarm system? That takes some advanced skill. And then to make a bonehead move like not wearing a disguise? Well, I never did mistake them for geniuses. But if they thought they were pulling a foolproof job, for instance, if they were told that the security system and cameras would be turned off, then they wouldn't have needed masks. Add it up and it gives some weight to the insurance scam plus frame-up theory."

"It sure does. Or they're just bad criminals. Can't always cover all the bases," Frank said. "Speaking of bases, it looks like the baseball team is still on the field." Frank pointed to the diamond as the van approached Shoreham High School.

"I wonder why they started practice a week before the other schools," Joe observed.

"They have a state championship to defend." Frank drove the van into the school's parking lot. Very few cars were there at this time of day, so Frank pulled into a spot close to the gym. From this vantage point, although they couldn't see the baseball diamond, they would be sure to see Rojas and Wingfoot leave the locker room after practice.

"Do you think we'll get anything out of them?" Frank asked.

"Why wait?" Joe replied. He got out of the van.

"Where are you going?" Frank followed his brother.

"To snoop. Maybe our two electronics wizards—the ones not savvy enough to wear masks to a robbery—have something hidden in their lockers."

Frank smiled as he followed his brother into the gym. A few people were playing basketball on the center court, a few others were in the weight room, and still others were just milling about. Nobody paid much attention to the Hardys.

Joe walked through the doors of the locker room, his brother following closely. Joe quickly scanned the locker room. There didn't appear to be anybody in there, and the showers were also silent.

"Check the nameplates," he whispered to Frank. "You take the back rows."

The two split up, Joe quickly walking down the first row of lockers while Frank sprinted to the back of the room.

After just two minutes of fruitless reading, Joe heard a whistle. He looked down the line of lockers. Frank was a few rows away, giving the thumbs-up sign. Joe quickly joined his brother.

"Rojas and Wingfoot," Frank said as he pointed at two lockers, "side by side."

"That makes it easy. Good thing they're best friends."

Frank reached into his pants pocket. He took out a long, thin metal pin with a hook at one end, along with a second, thicker rod.

"Good thing they don't use combination locks," Frank responded. He stuck the two pins into the lock that held Rojas's locker closed. After a few jiggles, the lock mechanism yielded to Frank's expert touch. Joe immediately began searching through the locker while Frank went to work on Wingfoot's lock.

"Find anything?" Frank asked as he began his search of Wingfoot's possessions.

"Just a goofy picture," Joe replied. "Here, look at this."

Frank glanced over to see what his brother was holding.

"'To some great performers. You're the best, Monty Andrews,'" Frank read. Joe had found a picture of Rojas and Wingfoot posing with the host of *Monty Mania.* "Looks like they were picked from the audience at one of the tapings."

Frank stuck his head inside Wingfoot's locker. Joe replaced the picture on the inside of the door to Rojas's locker. Then he closed the door and latched the lock.

"Bingo," Frank exhaled. Joe kneeled down to get a look at what had gotten Frank's attention.

"What have we here?" Joe asked with a smile.

"Gee," came a booming voice from behind the brothers, "we were just going to ask the same thing!"

8 Wanted Men

Frank and Joe stood up slowly. Frank still held the object that had riveted his attention before they were startled by the booming voice behind them. Joe gave his brother a what-do-we-do-now look as they calmly turned to face the guy, who was backed up by the Shoreham High School baseball team.

There was a moment of tense silence. Frank counted the number of people they faced—thirteen to two, not very good odds.

"I'll ask again," said a tall, lanky boy with dark skin and an angular face. "What do we have here?"

"Looks like a couple of thieves!" shouted a voice from the back of the pack of boys.

"Looks like a couple of Bayport bums, come here to sabotage us," another voice said.

"Yeah, I recognize them," said the dark-skinned teen. "You two play for Bayport High's baseball team. The Hardy brothers."

"And you're Pepper Wingfoot, and it looks like you're guilty," Joe responded. He pointed to what was clenched in Frank's hand. The older Hardy dangled a bright gold necklace between two fingers. The necklace had a heart-shaped charm that bore a small, sparkling diamond.

"Hey!" Wingfoot spat. "Where'd you get that necklace?" Wingfoot lunged forward to swipe the necklace from Frank's hand, but Frank clenched his fist and pulled the bauble out of reach.

"The real question should be, where did you get it?" Frank said. "Been doing some after-hours shopping?"

"Don't answer that," said the boy next to Pepper. He was as tall as Wingfoot but much more muscular. "We don't have to answer any questions about that."

"What are you hiding, Rojas?" Joe asked as he realized who the other boy was.

"Enough with the talk!" shouted another ballplayer. "Let's teach these Bayport goons a lesson."

"Yeah!" grumbled some of the other players as they descended on Frank and Joe. The brothers both put their hands in front of them.

"Come on, now," Frank said. "We didn't come here for a fight."

"Well, it looks like you found one," Rojas responded. He raised his fist, aiming it at Joe, who crossed his arms in front of his body in a defensive posture.

The punch, however, was halted by a loud voice instead.

"What are you guys all crowded around for?" asked a man in a Shoreham baseball uniform as he pushed through the crowd.

"These guys from Bayport broke in here and ransacked our lockers, Coach," Wingfoot explained.

The coach glared at Frank and Joe. Then he glanced at Rojas, who still had his fist cocked.

"Relax, Roberto," the coach said. "You don't need any more trouble."

"That's what we're here about," Frank said, holding up the jeweled necklace he had found in Pepper Wingfoot's gym bag.

The coach's eyes widened. He glanced at the crowd of ballplayers.

"Okay, hit the showers!" he growled. The crowd began to disperse, murmuring threats at Frank and Joe.

"You two come with me," the coach said to the Hardys. "You guys also." He indicated Rojas and Wingfoot. The four teens glared as they walked in silence behind the coach. He led them to a small office at the front of the locker room. When he was sitting behind his desk, he addressed the boys.

"One at a time, starting with you," he said pointing to Frank. "Names and explanations."

"I'm Frank Hardy, and this is my brother, Joe," Frank began. "We came here hoping to get some information from Rojas and Wingfoot about the robbery at the Jewelry Exchange."

"By breaking into my locker?" Wingfoot asked angrily.

"We wanted to see if you really were involved in that crime," Frank said.

"And I guess we found our answer," Joe added, indicating the necklace in his brother's hand.

"Let me see that," the coach said to Frank, who handed the necklace across the desk.

"Can you explain this?" he said to Wingfoot.

"Hey, maybe those guys planted it!" Rojas interjected.

Wingfoot shook his head. "Nice try at a save, buddy. But the truth will serve us better here. I bought it for my girlfriend a few weeks ago. I was saving it for her birthday."

"In your locker?" Joe asked with skepticism.

"After we were, you know, arrested, I moved it here so if the cops searched my house, they wouldn't be suspicious like you guys are now."

"Why wasn't it gift wrapped?" Frank asked.

"I was going to slip it around her neck. Figured it was cooler than just handing her a box with a ribbon around it."

"Do you have proof that you bought this necklace, Pepper?" the coach asked.

"Sure, Coach," Wingfoot replied. "I have a receipt and everything. Guess I didn't want any more hassle from the cops so I stashed it here."

"That's good enough for me," the coach said. He glared at Frank and Joe. "So, what's your interest in all of this. You work for the cops? Or maybe the jewelry store?"

"Neither," Joe said. "We're working for our girlfriends."

"See, they came to steal the necklace," Rojas said.

"How would we know there was even a necklace in there?" Joe replied. "We were looking for evidence."

"Why?

"Well, because our girlfriends, Iola Morton and Callie Shaw, were arrested for robbery, and we think it's tied into the break-in at the Jewelry Exchange," Joe explained.

"So your girls are doing time for a crime they tried to frame us for? Good."

"It's not like that, Rojas," Frank replied. "Look, we know they're innocent. Maybe you two are framing them for something you did."

"We didn't do anything," Wingfoot said. "Man,

I can respect you guys trying to help your girlfriends, but we have nothing to say to you that we haven't said already to the cops."

"Hey," Rojas said, cutting off his friend, "our lawyer told us to follow what the police told us and not say anything to anybody."

"Forget the rules," Wingfoot said. "These guys bent the rules to help their girlfriends. Maybe they can help us."

"If you're innocent," Joe said, "anything we do to help Iola and Callie will help you."

"There's nothing to help with," Rojas said. "We have no alibi, some stupid videotape puts us at the scene. Our meat is burned."

"Where were you two the night of the robbery?" Frank asked.

Wingfoot laughed. "That's the problem," he said. "We were just with each other, hanging in the woods outside of town. No witnesses, nothing."

"That's the only excuse Callie and Iola have, too."

There was nothing more to get from Rojas and Wingfoot. Frank and Joe apologized for breaking into their lockers.

"I'll let you two go this time with just a warning," the coach said. "But the only time or place I ever want to see you around here is on the field for a ball game. Understood?"

"Yes, sir," Joe said.

"Thank you, sir," Frank added.

The Hardys left Shoreham High School and started the long drive home.

"Drive by Callie's house. We can see if Mr. Shaw has any information after his trip to the police station," Frank said.

Joe followed his brother's instructions. When they arrived at the Shaw residence, there were several cars parked in the driveway. The Hardys recognized the cars belonging to the Shaws, as well as two owned by the Mortons. However, they had no idea who owned the expensive black foreign luxury car.

Frank knocked on the door. It opened almost instantaneously, as if their arrival was expected.

"Oh, Frank!" Callie shouted with glee as she grabbed her boyfriend around the waist. Frank returned Callie's hug. Joe nudged past the two to get to Iola, who was in the entryway.

"We're so glad to see you two," Joe said. "How'd you get bail set so quickly?"

"Don't answer that," Mr. Morton shouted from the living room. "Don't tell them anything."

"Dad!" Iola said angrily as the teens entered the living room. "Enough with this gag order."

"Your father is correct," said a man in a black suit. He was seated on the couch. On the coffee table in front of him rested an open briefcase, a yellow notepad, and several documents.

"And you are?" Joe asked.

"Stelfreeze. Brady Stelfreeze, attorney. I'm how bail was set so promptly. But that is the only thing you'll be told. Anything else these girls tell you will only hurt their chances in court."

"Why is everybody over the age of eighteen so determined to keep us from speaking with our friends?" Iola asked.

"Teen gangs," Frank said.

"Huh?"

Joe explained. "The way we figure it, the police think there is some sort of teen gang committing robberies."

"How do you know any of this?" Stelfreeze asked incredulously.

"Because they're better than any police detectives," Callie told him.

"And we think that they're our best chance to solve any mystery that involves other people our age, like those two boys from the Jewelry Exchange," Iola added.

"Rojas and Wingfoot," Frank said. "We just left them."

"Did you learn anything?" Stelfreeze asked.

"You first," Joe replied.

Stelfreeze said nothing.

"I'll break the stalemate," Iola said. "We were arrested for robbing the Golden Palace Jewelry Store."

"Iola!" Mr. Morton shouted.

"So they don't directly tie you into the Jewelry Exchange? Interesting."

"Frank, I don't think you're helping matters here," Mrs. Shaw said.

"I think they can," Mr. Shaw said. "I saw them at the police station. And to tell you the truth, they probably work faster and better than the cops I met down there."

"Thanks for the confidence," Frank said. He turned to Callie. "So why did the police come after you?"

"Supposedly they have us on videotape robbing the store last night."

"You have that tape?"

"A copy is being delivered to my office later today," Stelfreeze said.

"Frank," Joe said. "It's almost six o'clock. I say we hit the scene of the crime before the store closes."

"Good thinking. It's always a good idea to look for clues while the trail is warm."

Frank and Joe said goodbye and headed to the van. Twenty minutes later they were at the Golden Palace. The store was smaller than the Jewelry Exchange. It didn't even have its own parking lot. It was in the middle of the block, separated from the store to its left by an alleyway.

The brothers entered the Golden Palace, which was little more than a wide hallway with glass cases on one side and an office in back. The glass cases were all empty.

"Can I help you?" asked an old man as he came out of the back room. "We're not really open."

"The door was unlocked," Frank said.

"I've had police in and out all day. Plus anybody who had something on pre-order who came to pick it up, not knowing we were cleaned out last night. You here to pick up something?"

"Not anymore, I guess," Joe said.

"Sorry. But you'll get a refund or replacement as soon as the insurance settles or the stuff is recovered."

"They got everything, huh? We shouldn't have ordered from a place with so little security."

"Hindsight is twenty-twenty," said the old man. "The security for this place is just that one camera." He pointed to a camera on the ceiling above the glass cases. "Didn't figure on needing more than that for a little place like this. And it did its job. Caught those thieves on tape."

"Guess it did," Joe said. "Well, thanks."

"Is that an Eye Spy camera?" Frank asked.

"Sure is," the man answered. "It worked like a charm."

The brothers left the store.

"Not many clues there," Joe said.

The brothers stood outside the Golden Palace for a moment debating what to do next. Just then the front door to the store opened and the old man came outside, struggling to lift a large plastic garbage bag.

"Need some help with that?" Frank asked.

"Sure could."

Joe took the heavy bag from the man. "Where does it go?"

"There's a Dumpster in the alley. Thanks."

"No problem," Frank said. The man went back into the store. Joe headed for the alley, with Frank a step behind.

"This thing is heavy," Joe said. "It sounds as though it has glass in it."

"Maybe from a case that was broken during the heist."

"Could be. Help me lift this up."

Frank took hold of the bag. The two heaved it higher to maneuver it over the rim of the Dumpster. Just as the bag cleared the top it ripped, raining glass, paper, and other debris on to the concrete.

"At least most of it stayed in the bag," Joe said as he stooped to scoop up the garbage from the walkway. Frank bent down to help him.

"Well, what do you know," Frank said as he sifted through the garbage. "Our good deed with the garbage is going to leave us smelling like roses."

9 Video Magic

"I think the smell of this garbage has made you lose your senses, Frank."

"Well, it certainly has made me giddy. Here, look at this." Frank held up a small piece of stiff paper, no bigger than an unfolded chewing-gum wrapper.

"Looks like a torn lottery ticket," Joe said, refraining from touching the dirty piece of paper. "Or a movie ticket stub."

"Close," Frank said. "It's a ticket stub for the *Monty Mania* show."

"So? There are probably hundreds of *Monty Mania* ticket stubs in garbage bags all over town. It's a popular attraction."

"But think about it," Frank said. "This stub is from last night's show. Now it's here at the same place that Callie and Iola are accused of robbing last night."

"So maybe we should put it back in the garbage. From where I'm standing, that ticket stub only makes Iola and Callie look guilty."

"Except, one—we know in our hearts they didn't do it; and two—this stub is not for the seats we were sitting in. In fact, it doesn't have a seat number."

"Like it was a special pass?"

"Possibly."

"So where does that lead us, Frank?"

"Remember what you found in Rojas's locker? That picture of him and Wingfoot with Monty Andrews?"

"I follow you. These two crimes are starting to link themselves to that TV show."

"Exactly," Frank said. "Let's head for the van to see if we can contact those guys."

"So you think it really might be them? Who did the robbery, I mean," Joe asked.

"Could be," Frank replied.

Frank and Joe went back to the van. They called telephone information and learned that there was only one listing for the name Wingfoot. They dialed the number on their cellular phone and were pleased with the results.

"Bingo," Frank said as he clicked off the phone. He hooked his seat belt and started the van.

"Where are we going?"

"Wingfoot's house. Turns out that he and Rojas were at the *Monty Mania* show before they supposedly robbed the Jewelry Exchange. And to top it all off, they were hypnotized, just like Callie and Iola."

"And that proves what? That everybody is innocent?" Joe asked.

"No, of course it doesn't. But it may lead us to a theory or to other suspects. Wingfoot has a copy of their performance on *Monty Mania.* Maybe it will give us some ideas."

"So we're counting them out as suspects?" Joe continued his questioning.

"Not all the way, Joe. But I'm willing to go innocent until proven guilty for them. They're being helpful. I'm not sure they'd help us if they were guilty."

Frank gunned the van and headed for Pepper Wingfoot's house. Ten minutes later they were standing in his living room. Roberto Rojas had joined them.

"How do you think this *Monty Mania* thing ties in to the robberies?" Rojas asked as Wingfoot cued up the videotape of the pair's appearance on the show.

"I'm not sure yet," Frank answered. "Part of detective work is taking a hunch and breathing life into it."

The four young men sat on the couch and

watched the videotape. While Wingfoot fast-forwarded through the stuff that didn't involve him and Rojas, Joe picked up a newspaper from the coffee table.

"Oh," he said, "this is yesterday's paper."

"Yeah," said Pepper. "I figure to keep it because the front page makes me famous. It's got a snapshot from the video surveillance camera catching me and Roberto in the act of something we didn't do."

Joe put the newspaper back down on the table and turned his attention to the videotape. As he watched Monty Andrews hypnotize the two Shoreham baseball stars, he was eerily reminded of what he had witnessed happening to Iola and Callie.

"You know," Frank said, "Monty's act is sort of the same every time. It must be that whole idea of seeing yourself or somebody you know on television that makes the show popular."

"Or maybe he's hypnotizing the whole world through the screen," Rojas said.

Everybody laughed nervously.

"Now, there's a scary thought," Frank said.

Pepper shivered. "The world would be doomed if somebody could actually do that."

"Pause the tape!" Joe suddenly shouted. Wingfoot clicked the remote control.

"Can you go back a few frames?"

"This is a cheap VCR," Wingfoot said. "The

best it can do is go forward and backward. I can't go frame by frame or slow motion."

Joe took the remote. "Here, let me reverse it a bit. There." Joe hit Pause, freezing a scene on the screen.

"What did he have you doing there?" he asked.

"He was asking me to act as if I was about to hit a home run," said Rojas.

Joe grabbed the newspaper from the table and went over to the television. He held up the picture on the front page that showed Rojas and Wingfoot in the Jewelry Exchange. In the picture, Rojas was swinging a large hammer at a glass case full of jewelry.

"Look familiar?" Joe asked.

"Yeah," Rojas said. "That's my home run swing. So?"

Joe didn't reply. Instead, he turned back to the videotape and hit Play.

"Let's watch a little more," he said.

After a few minutes Frank put up his hand. "There," he said.

Joe hit Pause on the remote again. On the screen, Wingfoot was kneeling down, motioning as though he were picking something up from the floor and putting it in an invisible bag.

"He had me believing I had hit a jackpot playing slot machines in Vegas," Pepper said. "You know, a big one, where money is pouring out onto the floor."

"Which looks vaguely like you picking up some jewels from the floor and putting them in a bag," Frank said. "Just like in this picture."

"You still haven't proved anything," Rojas said. "In fact, you're starting to make me feel like I am guilty."

"Are you?" Joe asked. "Is there something you want to get off your chest?"

"No!" Rojas shouted. "I'm telling you, we did not rob that store."

"We'll go with your word for now," Frank said. "You've been a lot of help. Can we borrow the video, Pepper?"

"Sure. Just don't lose it. I've never seen Rojas so funny before. We may need it for laughs in jail."

When he got back in the van, Frank used the phone to dial Callie's house. He spoke with her for a few minutes, then said goodbye and dialed another number. Ten minutes after a very heated conversation, Frank and Joe were standing in the office of Brady Stelfreeze.

"I still have my reservations about you two being involved in this case," Stelfreeze said with disdain. "But the girls want you involved, and Mr. Shaw trusts you, so I'm willing to take a chance for now."

"You won't regret it, Mr. Stelfreeze," Joe said.

"I hope not. Anyway, I have the tapes from the security cameras at both the Jewelry Exchange and the Golden Palace."

"Good," Frank said. "Let's see the tape of Callie and Iola, please."

Stelfreeze pushed a button on the desk in front of him. A cabinet across the room opened, revealing a large television. He pressed another button and the interior of the Golden Palace filled the screen. The brothers stood as they watched Callie and Iola slink in through the front door.

"Screwdriver," Joe said, narrating. "Look around. Spot the security camera . . ."

"Tape the lens, but the tape falls off," Frank said.

It ended there as the girls escaped when a police siren wailed in the distance.

"That should do it," Frank said.

"Do what? Land those two in jail is the only thing that video does."

"Not yet, Mr. Stelfreeze," Joe said. "Do you have a copy of the girls' appearance on *Monty Mania?*"

"Not yet."

"That doesn't matter," Frank said. "Callie said one was sent to her house today." Frank walked over to the VCR and ejected the videotape.

"Is this the other one?" Joe asked, pointing to a tape on Stelfreeze's desk. The lawyer nodded his head as Joe picked up the tape.

"Good," Frank said. "It's getting late, and we have work to do. What time can you be at our house tomorrow?"

Stelfreeze got a confused look on his face. "Me? Tomorrow's Saturday."

"So bill time and a half," Joe said. "Here's the address."

"Be early," Frank said. "Skip breakfast. Mom makes great pancakes."

Frank and Joe left the lawyer's office, drove to Callie's house to pick up the video she had for them, and headed home. After a quick dinner, Frank asked Joe a favor.

"Could you disconnect the VCR from the television in the den?"

"Sure," Joe answered. "You have something cooking in that head of yours?"

"Bringing it to a boil, bro. Meet me in my room."

Joe retrieved the VCR and hauled it up to his brother's bedroom.

"Thanks," Frank said, taking the VCR from Joe and hooking it to his computer's video input connector.

For the next several hours, the brothers were huddled around the computer. The only interruption came at 1:00 A.M. when somebody knocked on Frank's partially shut door.

"It's getting very late, boys," said Mrs. Hardy, poking her head into the room. "Maybe you should call it a night."

"We're onto something very important, Mom,"

Frank replied. "It could help clear Callie and Iola."

Mrs. Hardy smiled and retreated without a word. A few minutes later she returned with a tray of snacks and juice to take her sons through what would be a night of hard work.

When Frank and Joe came down to breakfast the next morning, Brady Stelfreeze was helping himself to some maple syrup.

"Enjoy your breakfast," Frank said as he pulled up a chair. "It's just the start to what should be a great day."

"Well, the breakfast is wonderful," Mr. Stelfreeze said with a smile. "So, I won't consider this a wasted trip."

"Oh, it won't be, we promise," Joe said.

After twenty minutes of eating and small talk, Mr. Stelfreeze joined the brothers in Frank's bedroom.

"So, what did you want to show me?" he asked. "Your fingerprint kit?"

"Oh, something much more high-tech than that," Frank said. "Watch."

Joe pressed Play on the VCR. The computer monitor displayed Wingfoot and Rojas performing on *Monty Mania.* Then a thick black line split the screen in half, and the previously full-screen image was relegated to the left side of the monitor.

On the right side of the black line the screen showed footage of the two Shoreham students inside the Jewelry Exchange.

"Guilty, says the jury," Stelfreeze snickered. "All I see is some irrelevant video from a television variety show on the screen next to a solid piece of evidence proving that these two robbed the jewelry store. Is this all you have to show me?"

"How about this?" Frank said as he pushed a few keys on the computer. The black line that dissected the screen in two disappeared. The separate images began to expand and superimpose one on top of the other.

"Hmm," Stelfreeze mouthed with a bit of interest.

Frank clicked away some more at the keyboard. The images on the screen began to shift as if they were melting together. As the colors and lines swirled, a new image began to replace the pictures of Rojas and Wingfoot going about their crime. For a moment the screen was a jumble of body parts, backgrounds, and facial features.

"I think I see something," Stelfreeze said, staring at the fuzzy blob of colors. "But I'm not sure what."

Then the image on the monitor stabilized as the computer completed its computations.

"There you have it!" Frank said with pride. "The real criminal."

10 Flimsy Evidence

"I don't get it," Stelfreeze said. "You plan to use some fancy computer graphics to frame somebody else for the robberies?"

"No." Joe sighed. "We used the computer to show you how the real criminal framed Callie and Iola and Wingfoot and Rojas."

"So you think that Monty Andrews, host of America's latest favorite variety show, is the real criminal?" Stelfreeze asked, pointing at the picture of the comedian on the computer screen. "How do you come up with that?"

"Look at the screen," Frank said as he tapped a few keys. A side-by-side split-screen image from the Golden Palace video and the *Monty Mania* video twinkled on the monitor.

"Now, with a little magic of my own," Frank

said as he rolled the mouse around the pictures on the screen, outlining images and making them disappear, "I take Callie and Iola out of the *Monty Mania* video, drop them into the Golden Palace, do a little touch-up painting, and there you have it. Callie and Iola are actresses in whatever movie Monty Andrews wants them to star. With a touch of a button, I can even make the images move, just like a videotape."

"So you're trying to say that Monty Andrews robbed both of those stores, and he used a computer to splice together scenes from his television show into the video surveillance equipment. I don't think your evidence is very compelling."

"But you might be able to use it to create a reasonable doubt about the girls committing the crime," Joe said. "That would be enough to keep them out of jail."

"Sure, after a lengthy trial," Stelfreeze said. "I came here thinking you might be able to prove who the real criminal was."

"We did," Frank said.

"I need proof," Stelfreeze replied, "not speculation. Hard evidence."

"Oh, we'll get some hard evidence," Joe promised, "now that we know where to look."

Stelfreeze left the room, wishing the brothers good luck. Frank went about shutting down the computer. Joe grabbed a towel from the closet.

"Where are you going?" Frank asked.

"To take a shower. I want to be nice and fresh when we nail Monty Andrews."

After Joe finished his shower and Frank had a turn in the bathroom, the brothers headed out to the van.

Frank tossed Joe the keys. "You drive," he said. "You seem to have a destination in mind."

"Just basic detective work," Joe replied as he got in the van. "Start where the trail left off. For Monty Andrews, that would mean the television studio."

"On a Saturday?"

"Television is a twenty-four–seven operation. We'll pick up his scent there."

Thirty minutes later Joe was hushing his brother's applause.

"Thank you, thank you," Joe said as the van pulled into the station's parking lot.

"Man, Joe, your timing was great." Frank pointed to Monty Andrews as the entertainer emerged from the side door of the Bayport television studio.

"Hey, entertainment is all timing, bro. Now let's just sit here and see what that worm is up to."

Frank and Joe sat back while they watched Monty Andrews. The actor stood by the side door, reading what appeared to be a newspaper. Monty grimaced at what he saw. After another few seconds he crumpled the paper in a big wad and threw it into the trashcan. As soon as Monty walked away from the can, Joe edged the van slowly forward.

"Watch what car he gets in," Joe said. "I want to see what has him so riled."

Joe pulled up next to the trashcan, jumped out and grabbed the newspaper, and jumped right back in behind the wheel.

"Blue two-door sports car," Frank said as he took the paper from his brother.

"Got him," Joe responded. He put his foot on the gas and headed for the exit a few car lengths behind Monty Andrews.

"I guess Chief Collig couldn't keep this under wraps forever," Frank said with a laugh as he straightened the newspaper. "And I quote: 'Anonymous sources inside the police department say they are worried that a new wave of teen crime is coming to Bayport.' Then the article lays out some particulars from both jewelry heists."

"And such news would make Monty unhappy?" Joe said with disbelief. He kept the van a few cars behind the actor's sports car as Monty drove it toward the business district. "I'd think with the cops looking for a mysterious gang, he'd think he got away scot-free."

"Me, too. Unless he's afraid that somebody will put together the similarities between the 'thieves' the way we did."

The brothers drove in silence for a while, focusing their attention on the blue sports car. After a few minutes of weaving in and out of light downtown traffic, Monty pulled up in front of a large office building. Joe drove past Monty Andrews as the hypnotist got out of his car. Joe rolled the van to a stop a few cars in front of where Monty had parked.

"Maybe he's going to see his agent," Frank said as he exited the van.

"Or his lawyer. Stay back some. There's no crowd to blend into, and he might recognize us from the other night."

After Monty entered the office building, Frank and Joe sprinted to the door. They entered the building just in time to see the elevator door close. There weren't very many people in the building on an early Saturday morning.

"Tenth floor," Frank announced, pointing up at the floor indicator above the elevator. That was the only floor the elevator had stopped on.

Joe followed Frank onto a vacant elevator and hit the button marked Ten.

"Here's a building directory," Joe said. He pointed to a board next to the elevator controls. "Tenth floor has two lawyers, an advertising agency, and Eye Spy Security. That sounds familiar."

"Here's our stop," Frank said before the brothers could discuss anything further. The elevator doors opened, and Joe peeked into the hallway. He nodded to indicate that the coast was clear. Then he stepped out of the elevator and swiftly moved across the hallway. Frank followed him, and two seconds later both were kneeling behind a large plastic tree that was situated across from the bank of elevators.

Both Hardys scanned the hallway. To the left of them, about twenty feet from the elevator, the hall curved. On the wall was a sign indicating that the advertising agency was down that corridor. To the right, again twenty feet away, the hallway split in two. It forked to the left at a sign indicating the direction to the lawyers' offices. In front of the Hardys, fifty more feet away, the hall ended in a large double door. The sign read Eye Spy Security—Ronald Johnson, President. The door was slightly ajar. On the carpet, thin strips of light, painted with shifting shadows, proved that the office was occupied.

A familiar voice wafted angrily through the air.

"Look," the voice said, "I don't know what's going on here, but I know my own work when I see it. I don't want to get caught up in anything."

There was a pause. Then the sound of soft talking reached the brothers' ears. They strained to listen, but could not make out what was said. There was a silence that was followed by more undecipherable talking. Suddenly a loud "Hey!" was followed by a thud and then more silence.

Joe noticed that the light reflecting on the hallway carpet got a bit wider. He pushed himself and Frank lower behind the tree. Then three figures strode past them and waited by the elevators directly across from where they were hiding. Joe risked reaching up and parted some of the plastic branches. In the second he chanced a glance, he saw something that did not please him: a dazed-looking Monty Andrews was slumped between two large men in suits.

When the elevator arrived, the two men dragged Monty on board. After the door was closed, Joe peeked around the tree to make sure the coast was clear. The door to Eye Spy Security was still partially ajar. Frank looked at the numbers above the just departed elevator. The lights were moving up instead of down.

"They must be heading for the roof," Frank whispered. He got to his feet and darted across the hall to a door marked Exit.

Joe was right behind him as Frank entered the stairwell.

"Oh, now this is looking like a movie I don't want to star in," Joe said as he saw several flights of stairs unwind above him.

"It's great exercise," Frank replied as he started to dash up the stairs.

"Pace yourself," Joe said as he followed his older brother. "There are fifteen floors total in this building."

"Five flights is nothing. And Monty may not have time for us to pace ourselves."

Frank was right. As they reached the last landing and faced the door to the roof, they heard the sound of scuffling feet.

"No!" somebody shouted on the other side of the door. "Stop!"

11 Over the Edge

Frank was through the door first, and he hit the roof running with Joe at his heels.

"Uh, guys, you don't really want to do that," Joe said as he and Frank froze in their tracks about fifteen yards from the strongmen. "Very messy."

Both thugs looked over their shoulders at the intruders. Monty Andrews used the sudden distraction to wriggle from side to side, hoping to break free from his captors. However, neither of them loosened their grip on Andrews, who was standing at the edge of the roof, shivering with fright.

"We learned about this in physics," Frank added. "Mass, acceleration, *splat.*"

Not caring about the appearance of two teens, the thugs turned their attention back to Monty.

They pushed the struggling actor closer to the edge until one of his feet was over the side, dangling in midair.

"Here's something we learned in criminology," Joe said, raising his voice. "It's called murder witness."

The two thugs looked at each other. One let go of Monty and turned toward Joe. The other tightened his grip on Monty and dragged him back to solid ground. As soon as the television host's feet touched the roof, the thug slugged him hard in the stomach. Monty crumpled up like a candy wrapper and slumped to his knees, wheezing for air.

"Good, now that we have your attention," Joe said, "let's get down to cases. Attempted murder. Thug A is six-foot-six, two hundred twenty pounds, very short brown hair, muscular, and has the bad taste to wear brown shoes and a green shirt with a blue suit."

"Thug B," Frank said, picking up where his brother left off, "is six-foot-nine, two hundred thirty-nine pounds, has long blond hair in a ponytail, and is very tan. We have you made, gentlemen. If anything ever happens to him," Frank added, pointing to the prone form of Monty Andrews, "you are the prime suspects."

The two thugs clenched their fists. They smiled at each other and then took several slow steps toward Frank and Joe.

"I think we've made our point," Joe said as the bad guys cut the distance between them.

"I insist," Frank said, pointing to the door that led back into the building's stairwell. "After you."

Joe swung the door open and bolted into the stairwell. He was down a full flight of stairs by the time Frank even hit the first landing.

"Together or split?" Joe asked. He put his hand on the door that led to the fifteenth floor.

"Split," Frank called down to his brother. "I just want to make sure the fish are hooked."

Joe pulled open the door and headed into the hallway. He paused for a moment. He heard footsteps soar down the stairs behind the closing door. He figured that was Frank running past. Then Joe heard some lumbering steps. The footfalls paused on the landing.

"I'm in here!" Joe shouted. "Boy, you guys sure are not rocket scientists."

As soon as Joe finished his insult, the door flew open and the fashion-unconscious thug entered the hallway. Joe waved, turned, and sprinted down the hall in the opposite direction. He rounded the corner and shot down another corridor, glancing over his shoulder to make sure he was still being pursued. He was. Joe was satisfied that he had drawn the bad guy away from Monty Andrews. He picked up his pace and turned another corner.

* * *

Meanwhile, Frank led the tan thug on a tiring chase down the stairwell.

"Ah, seven," Frank read from a sign on the wall of the next landing. "Lucky number." Frank opened the stairwell door and entered the seventh-floor hallway. He sprinted to the elevator and pressed the down button. Just as the car arrived, his pursuer entered the hallway.

"Fifth floor," Frank called out to his pursuer as he entered the elevator. "You'll have to take the stairs." The elevator door closed, leaving the thug to growl and turn back to the stairwell.

Frank emerged on the fifth floor. He leaned casually against the wall. A minute later the tan thug burst through the stairwell door.

"Tired already? They just don't build bad guys like they used to."

The thug stood his ground and fixed Frank with an icy glare. He reached into his sports coat and drew out a long-barreled pistol.

"Now, this is supposed to be a friendly game," Frank protested. "Besides, gunshots bring more witnesses."

The thug shook his head with disappointment. He put the gun back in his jacket.

"That's better. Shall we?" Frank sprinted down the hallway. He saw the exit for another stairwell, pointed his intention out to his pursuer, and slammed through the door.

Frank chanced a peek over his shoulder. He was

rapidly putting floors between himself and the thug chasing him.

Frank burst through the door in front of him and found himself on the first floor. Unlike the other floors, which contained office suites, this floor was open and airy, nothing more than a square of corridors surrounded in the center by a rail that looked down on the lobby atrium.

Frank glanced around. There was a café and a newspaper stand just to his left. Both were open, although very few people were around on a Saturday. Frank reached into his pocket, grabbed two quarters, and put them on the counter of the newsstand. He picked up a copy of the morning paper. Then he walked into the café and sat down in a booth against the wall just left of the entryway. He unfolded the newspaper and held it up in front of his face.

A waiter came over immediately.

"Just a root beer," Frank said from behind the paper. "I'm waiting for somebody." The waiter went into the kitchen.

Frank peered stealthily over the top of his newspaper. Only a few people passed by the front of the café, none of them the tan thug. Frank's drink came. He took a few sips behind the newspaper.

"Will there be anything else?" the waiter asked.

"Nope, looks like my friend isn't going to make it." Frank put down the newspaper, took two dollars out of his pocket, and plopped the money on the table. He walked to the café entryway and cautiously peeked into the hallway. Satisfied that he had given his pursuer the slip, Frank walked over to the bank of elevators and pressed the up button.

While Frank was using the whole building for his game of cat and mouse, Joe kept his chase confined to a smaller area. He used his speed to stay ahead of his pursuer. Unfortunately, when Joe entered the ninth-floor stairwell, he had picked up two tails.

"Aww, does that mean you can't find my brother?" Joe said to the tan thug. "I'll try to move more slowly for you." Then Joe poured on the speed and sprinted up the stairs. Both thugs lumbered several yards behind him.

If Frank wiggled free, Joe thought, there's only one place he's going. Sure enough, as Joe led his two chasers on a grueling climb of flight after flight of stairs, Joe heard a groan ahead of him.

"What hit me?" a voice said. There was the sound of footsteps a flight above Joe.

"Frank!" Joe called as he ran. "I want to lose these guys for good."

"Up here!" Frank called to his brother. When Joe hit the next landing, he went through the stairwell door and into the hallway on the thirteenth floor. Just ahead of him, he saw Frank standing at the bank of elevators, Monty Andrews leaning heavily against him. Joe sprinted to join his brother. As he reached the elevators, he could see that Frank was pressing the button so that both cars were held open. Joe stuck his head into the car on the left and pressed the buttons for every floor. Then he got into the other elevator car with his brother and Monty Andrews. Frank continued to hold both elevators open.

Two seconds later both thugs came into the hallway.

"We held the elevator for you," Frank called as he let go of the button. He ducked his head inside the right-hand elevator car as the door began to close. The poorly dressed thug reached the bank of elevators just as both doors closed.

"You could always take the stairs!" Joe hollered. Then he slumped against the wall, letting his hot muscles unwind.

"Do you think we lost them?" Frank asked.

"Thirteen more flights of running stairs?" Joe replied. "They probably gave up for now."

When the elevator reached the lobby, Frank cautiously poked his head out into the corridor.

"Coast looks clear," he said, taking a wary step out of the elevator. He looked around again. Satisfied that the two thugs had not yet reached the ground floor, Frank motioned to his brother.

When the trio made it out of the building, Frank led the still groggy television celebrity to the van.

He pushed Monty inside, and then he and Joe got in. Joe started the engine and pulled out into the sparse downtown traffic.

"Okay, time to answer some questions," Frank said to Monty Andrews.

"Wha . . . Who . . ." Monty rubbed his abdomen. "Hey, you're those two—wait, I never forget a face."

"The Hardys," Joe said.

"Yeah." Monty snapped his fingers. "The kid detectives from the show." Monty suddenly turned pale. "Hey! Where are you taking me?" he asked with a shaky voice.

Frank and Joe remained silent, letting the fear grow in the entertainer.

"What do you want with me?" Monty ventured.

"To confess to robbing those jewelry stores!" Joe spat.

"I was afraid this was going to happen," Monty said, trembling.

"What, that you'd get caught?" Frank asked.

"No, that I'd get blamed." Monty hung his head in shame.

"You'd better start making some sense," Joe threatened.

"I-I'm not behind those robberies," Monty stammered. "But I think I may be responsible."

Frank stared icily at the television star. Monty gulped.

"Come on, what are you going to do to me?" he asked, but the brothers remained silent.

"Okay, look," Monty said. "I think the real thief is Ronald Johnson. I think he set me up."

"So far the only people who've been set up are some friends of ours," Joe said.

"Johnson," Frank cut in. "He owns Eye Spy Security."

"That's right," Monty replied. "That's where I was when those goons, Louie Spicolli and Larry Zybysko, grabbed me. I went there because I saw the newspaper and I realized that both sets of teens that landed in jail had been hypnotized by me the evenings of the robberies. I think Johnson is using them somehow to make these heists. When I confronted him, Johnson unleashed Spicolli and Zybysko."

"So far you both sound guilty," Joe said. "What's your connection to Johnson?"

"I'm into him for a lot of money. The guy's a loan shark. He kept letting me run up the interest on my loan. Then when I hit it big with *Monty Mania,* he decided to call in the marker. But by then my debt was huge, much more than I could pay all at once. He made me a deal."

"And what was the deal?" Frank asked.

"He wanted me to give some of the people I hypnotized special instructions. It was purely by chance whom he chose. Or so I thought. Now I'm thinking there was something particular about these people, but I don't know what."

"The teen gang theory," Joe stated. Frank nodded in agreement.

"What? Anyway, sometimes Johnson would coach me before the show on how he wanted me to do my routines. He wanted a lot of young guests. And he wanted the hypnotism routines to contain a lot of mystery and action. It sounded like good, solid entertainment, so I integrated his suggestions into the act. Anyway, after some performances, he would meet me backstage and have me give posthypnotic instructions to some of the guests."

"What were the instructions?" Frank asked.

"Seemed innocent enough. He wanted them to go to the park, make sure that nobody followed them, and to stay out of sight for several hours. He told me to do it, and I didn't ask any questions. He owns me!"

"So how does this all fit together?" Joe asked. "Ronald Johnson, legitimate businessman and loan shark, uses a two-bit hypnotist to give innocent teenagers weird instructions on what to do onstage and where to go later that night. I'm not sure I'm buying any of this."

"I don't know how this ties into the robberies," Monty said. "Maybe Johnson goes to the park and snatches the kids and uses the influence of my hypnosis to get them to hit the stores."

"Great," Frank said. "The hypnotism probably doesn't leave any telltale traces that can be used to prove the robbers weren't in their right minds when they did the crime."

"So, we know how Johnson might be doing it," Joe said, "but that doesn't help us catch him."

"Oh, yes it does," Frank said as the van pulled into the television station parking lot. "It gives me an idea on how to nail Ronald Johnson at his own game."

12 Caught in the Act

"So how do we nail him?" Joe asked.

"He's looking for actors." Frank smirked. "Teenage actors. Like us."

Joe gave his brother a questioning look. Then he nodded his head.

"So where do I fit in?" Monty asked.

"You're going to put us on your show," Frank said.

"What!" Joe was taken by surprise by his brother's request. But he immediately recovered and backed up his brother. "What a great idea."

"We'll be your next teens chosen from the audience," Frank explained. "Then let's see if this Ronald Johnson comes after us."

Joe stopped the van at the back door to the television studio.

"Are we agreed?" he asked.

"Okay, sure." Monty reached into his jacket and pulled out two tickets to his show. "I guess I owe you guys for saving me up on that roof. You're on Monday."

"Good," Frank said. "Make it four tickets." The performer produced two more tickets. Frank opened the van door and let Monty out onto the sidewalk.

"Just for the record," Joe said, "which goon is which?"

"Zybysko's the one with the tan," Monty replied.

"Thanks," Joe said.

"Hey, what about my car?" Monty cried. "It's still downtown. And what if Spicolli and Zybysko try to grab me again."

"Catch a cab to get the car," Joe shouted as he put the van in gear. "And as for those two goons, I doubt they'll be after you again. Johnson probably just wanted them to scare you."

When they were away from the studio, Joe questioned his brother.

"Why do we want to be on the show?"

"Because it's the best way to see how things operate around there. And I want to stick close to Monty."

"So you don't buy the whole Ronald Johnson story?" Joe asked.

"I buy into most of it," Frank replied. "But I think Monty's in it with him."

"But now Monty's scared that Johnson will have him killed," Joe said.

"Hey, robbery and frame-up is a dirty business. But big money makes for strange partners. I figure Monty will be back in on the scam either to make more dough or to save his own hide."

The Hardy brothers spent the rest of the weekend in relative serenity. They checked in on Callie and Iola and brought the girls up to speed on their investigation. The rest of the weekend was spent doing homework and catching up on lost sleep, except for the time Frank did a background check on Ronald Johnson.

Frank fired up the computer Sunday night and surfed the Internet. He visited Eye Spy Security's Web site, where he learned that the company provided security for countless businesses in Bayport. Their systems were state of the art. In fact, Eye Spy prided itself on using cameras of such high quality that even some television studios used them for inexpensive video filming.

"I wouldn't be surprised to learn later that Eye Spy Security provides cameras for the *Monty Mania* production," Frank speculated. "That would give Johnson fast access to the film he wanted to splice into the surveillance camera footage at the stores."

As for Ronald Johnson himself, there was very little to be learned. He had graduated from a small-town business college, had no police record, and supposedly built Eye Spy from scratch. Some intense creative research did unveil that he was a distant relative of a small-time New York crime boss, but other than blood, there was nothing to tie Ronald Johnson into anything shady.

"Still," Joe pointed out, "that could be where the loan shark money originally came from. Then he turned that money into Eye Spy."

"Possibly. And being a security expert would help him get inside any place he wanted to rob. Especially places for which he provided the security system."

At school on Monday, Frank and Joe gathered Callie, the Mortons, and Tony Prito together. The group sat in the cafeteria at their usual table by the window.

"Okay, the timing is going to be tight," Joe said. "We have baseball practice after school, so Frank and I will have to rush over to the station." He took two tickets out of his pocket and handed one to Chet and one to Tony. "You two meet us inside. Get there early and see if you can get close to Monty Andrews, like you're autograph hounds or something. Better yet, say you're doing a story for the school newspaper. He's such a ham, you might be able to get him talking. Maybe you can pick up some buzz backstage."

"Hey, where are our tickets?" Iola asked.

"At first we were thinking Callie and Iola would go to the show with us," Frank replied. "But I think seeing two of his former victims might spook Monty or Ronald Johnson."

"So we get left out in the cold?" Callie sounded very disappointed.

"Exactly," Frank said. "We need you to park and hold the space next to you for us. Then we want you stationed at that back entrance to the studio, where the guests come out after the show."

"This is important," Joe continued. "You're our safety net. If we're given a posthypnotic suggestion to get out of sight for a while, your job is to stay right on top of us wherever we go."

"Should we go with you in the van?" Iola asked.

"No," Joe said. "Just in case the crooks are keeping tabs on us to make sure they can pull off a robbery, we want them to think they're in the clear. You'll have to be very discreet in following us."

"What should Tony and I do after the show?" Chet asked.

"Go to our house and wait for us there," Frank replied. "If the setup is anything like what happened with Callie and Iola, we'll be long gone from the studio before you could get outside to your car. But our house will give you a base from which to back all of us up if we need you."

With the plans wrapped up, they all went their separate ways for the afternoon. They met for one more pep talk after classes. Then Frank and Joe went to baseball practice. A grueling two hours later, the Hardys were in the locker room, washing their aching muscles in the shower.

"Man, the coach sure put us through some workout for the first day," Joe said.

"Yeah," Frank agreed. "He found out that Shoreham started practice last week, so he wants to make up for lost time."

The brothers finished their showers, got dressed, and drove over to the television studio. The parking lot was almost completely full. They circled the rows of cars until they found Callie and Iola, standing in an empty parking space next to Callie's car.

"People must have loved you two," Joe said. "This is the last spot."

"A wink and a smile does wonders," Callie replied. "Even for some poor guy looking for a parking space."

The brothers ran into the studio while the girls took up their station by the back door of the building.

Inside, Frank and Joe found their seats next to Tony and Chet.

"Get anything?" Frank asked.

"Some autographed pictures," Tony said. "And a look at somebody we think is Ronald Johnson."

"Black hair, small pug nose, wide, round blue eyes?" asked Frank.

"Yeah," Chet replied.

"That's him," Frank said. "His picture was on the Eye Spy Web site."

"Yeah, well, as soon as he showed up, Monty shooed off the fans who were backstage. Johnson wanted to talk to him. Monty didn't look happy."

"That could be a good sign," Joe said. "Maybe Johnson wants to pull another heist tonight."

The house lights dimmed, and the show started. After the assistant producer went through the show's rules, Monty came out and did his opening routine. Then, just as planned, when it came time to pick participants from the audience, he zeroed in on Frank and Joe.

"Hey, we have some repeat performers!" Monty beamed. "I recognize you guys from last week." Monty zipped into the audience and stood next to Frank.

"Come on, audience, let's see if we can get these two . . . What were your names again?" Monty stuck the microphone in Joe's face.

"Joe and Frank Hardy."

"Let's see if we can get Joe and Frank to let us hypnotize them."

The audience erupted in applause. Monty began to walk down the aisle. Frank and Joe followed him to the stage. After some questions and jokes, Monty hypnotized the two brothers.

"Now, those of you who tuned in last week may remember that these young boys fancy themselves superdetectives. Well, let's see how they feel when the shoe is on the other foot."

Monty turned to Frank and Joe. "It's time for some cops and robbers," he said as he motioned to somebody offstage. A crew rolled out some props, and the stage suddenly looked like a warehouse.

"Okay, think of some of the crooks you've caught in the past. Now use this warehouse to replay some of their dastardly schemes."

Frank and Joe went to the warehouse set. First, Frank produced a set of lock picks from his back pocket and worked on the warehouse door. Once inside, the brothers skulked around, melting into pretend shadows. Joe tore open one of the prop boxes, got a greedy look on his face, and reached inside. Then he held his hands up as if he were showing something to Frank. Frank went to the back of the warehouse and pulled an imaginary chain as though he were opening a loading-dock door. Then Frank and Joe began lifting some of the prop boxes as if they were loading the stolen goods into a truck.

The audience howled with delight at how Monty Andrews had gotten the two do-gooders to commit a "crime." Monty then snapped Frank and

Joe out of their trances and sent them backstage. They signed some legal release forms and were then met by Monty Andrews after he wrapped up the show.

A little while later Frank and Joe walked out the backstage door.

"How'd it go?" Callie asked when the two had emerged from the building.

"Uh, okay," Frank stammered as he walked past his girlfriend. Joe completely ignored Iola as he followed his older brother.

"Posthypnotic suggestion," Iola whispered to Callie. "Let's stay on them."

Frank and Joe walked to the van. The girls hung back a little to make sure that somebody else wasn't watching them watch their boyfriends.

Frank got in the driver's seat, but he didn't start the engine for a few minutes. Then the passenger door opened and closed. Frank started the engine. As he pulled out of the parking space, he saw Callie and Iola jump into their car. He could just make out the sound of Callie's engine vainly struggling to start as the people who were supposed to keep tabs on him and Joe became smaller and smaller in the rearview mirror.

13 The Disappearing Hardys

It wasn't until after eleven that evening that Frank and Joe Hardy saw anybody else. The brothers entered their house. Inside, the living room was full of people. Mrs. Hardy carried in a tray of refreshments while Fenton Hardy sat on the couch stoically comforting the guests. Callie paced the floor; Iola wrung her hands; and Chet and Tony pulled books off the shelf above the television, trying to keep themselves distracted.

Frank and Joe glanced at the gathering for a moment and then wordlessly began to ascend the stairs.

"Hold it right there!" Callie shouted. Frank and Joe both froze in their tracks. "Come down here." Both young men followed the terse instructions.

"Okay, what's the big idea?" Callie asked.

Frank and Joe stared at her with blank expressions.

"Let's ease up a second," Fenton Hardy suggested. "If what you told me about the hypnotism is correct, they may not answer such vague questions."

"Let me try," Tony said. "How about 'Frank and Joe, where have you been this evening since you left the studio?' "

"We drove to the lake," Frank stated.

"Well, we were supposed to follow you to verify that," Iola said. "But when we got in Callie's car, it wouldn't start. We had to call the automobile club to help us. Turns out somebody jammed the starter."

"Did you do that, Joe?" Callie asked.

"Yes," he answered.

"Why?"

"Because we wanted to be alone," Frank answered.

"Well, they were probably instructed to make sure they weren't followed," Chet offered. "And seeing as they had prior plans to be followed, Joe sabotaged Callie's car so that couldn't happen."

"So that solves that mystery," Fenton said. "Now, from what you kids said about Callie and Iola's experience, the boys probably won't recall enough to be of any help. They'll probably be pretty out of it until tomorrow."

"In that case," Mrs. Hardy said, "everybody

should go on home and get some sleep. You do have school tomorrow."

"Sleep?" Iola asked, agitated. "Who's going to get any sleep after all of this?"

"I'm always good for a night's sleep," Tony offered with a smile.

"Come on," Chet said, "I'll give everybody a ride home."

The next morning Frank and Joe were a little sluggish getting out of bed.

"I feel like a big wad of cotton is where my brain used to be," Frank said.

"I'm a bit out of it also," Joe replied.

The brothers washed up and got ready for school in silence. They had a quick breakfast and were out the door without so much as a "good morning" to their parents. They got in the van and drove to the school, saying nothing to each other.

Several blocks away from the school, Frank finally perked up a little bit. A black sedan accelerated past them on the passenger side of the van. Then, just as the car pulled ahead of the van, it swerved to the side and screeched to a halt perpendicular to the Hardy vehicle. Frank slammed down hard on the brakes, and the van slid to a stop just a few feet away from the sedan.

"What's going on!" Joe yelled out his window. Then he caught sight of a familiar man getting out of the car. "Zybysko," Joe said. He reached for his door handle and got out of the van, not bothering to close the door. Frank followed suit. In seconds the two brothers stood in front of their van, ready for action.

Zybysko hung back a moment until he was joined by Spicolli. Then they approached the Hardys.

"Look," Frank said, "enough is enough. We don't have time for this. We're just a couple of kids who were in the wrong place at the wrong time."

"Can't we all just be friends?" Joe asked. "We could give you some fashion tips."

"Oh, that helped," Frank said. The two thugs came right up to Frank and Joe. Spicolli grabbed Joe's shirt collar.

"Hey, let him go," Frank said as he grabbed his brother's attacker's arm. Zybysko grabbed Frank and pushed him up against the van.

Instinct took over in both teens. Joe thrust his arms forward and up between his assailant's arms applying fast pressure to the man's elbow joints. The thug let go. Joe took the opportunity to drive his shoulder into the man's midsection.

Frank grabbed Zybysko's wrist and twisted, forcing the thug to release his hold on his neck. Then Frank used his leverage to force the larger man to the ground. When Zybysko's face reached Frank's midsection, Frank kicked him. The force of the blow started a trickle of blood from the thug's tan nose.

Free of their attackers, Frank and Joe scrambled for the van. But just as Joe climbed into the passenger seat, Spicolli grabbed him. Joe kicked his legs and connected with his attacker's shoulder. Spicolli let go, and Joe pulled his door shut.

"Hit it, Frank!" Frank threw the van into reverse and gunned the engine. The van was halfway down the block before the thugs even reached their car. Frank twisted the steering wheel. The van spun one hundred eighty degrees. Then Frank switched gears, hit the gas, and sped away.

"Should we report the incident?" Frank asked.

"What's to report? That we easily escaped two inept bad guys for the second time? Why bother?"

"Yeah, it was easy, wasn't it," Frank agreed. Joe laughed.

After that, the rest of the day was pleasantly quiet. Frank and Joe met with their friends during lunch, but had little insight to offer about their activities from the prior night.

"We'll just have to see if anything develops," Frank said, picking over the cafeteria's special of the day.

"And if something doesn't happen soon to give us a break in this case," Joe added, "we'll start looking for another way to clear you two."

"Thanks, guys," Iola said.

"We know we can count on you," Callie added.

School wrapped up for the day, and Frank and

Joe headed for the locker room. It was the first day of baseball season, and Bayport High School's first challenge was to host the defending state champions, Shoreham High.

The mood in the locker room was cheerful as the players psyched themselves up to take on their rivals. Everyone dressed quickly and headed out to the field to stretch and warm up. Frank was scheduled to pitch the opening-day game, so he headed to the pitcher's mound to get a feel for the diamond. Joe stepped up to the plate with a bat in his hand.

"Throw some warm-up pitches," he hollered to Frank. "I'll use them for batting practice while we wait for Coach Tarkanian."

Frank threw some pitches. The first ones were soft and straight as he loosened his muscles, so Joe put those balls into orbit. Then Frank got serious. He threw his patented Hardy Heater, smoking the fastball past his brother.

"There you go, bro," Joe said. "Looking good."

After a few more pitches and swings, some strikes and some hits, the brothers headed for the dugout.

The entire team gathered together. As they high-fived and whooped it up a bit, the Shoreham team took to the field to warm up.

"I wonder where Coach Tark is," Joe said.

"He was in his office talking to somebody," a

teammate said. "The blinds were pulled so I couldn't see who. But the coach didn't sound happy."

"Ah, probably nothing," Frank said, trying to keep his teammates loose. Then Frank turned to the team's catcher to discuss the pitch signs and strategy.

"Frank, Joe," a voice boomed suddenly. The players all looked at the dugout entrance, which was filled by the form of their coach.

"Yes, Coach," Frank said.

"You two get on over to the locker room. Somebody there to see you."

"What's up?" Joe asked. "The game's going to start soon."

"I know," the coach replied. "You two are scrubbed for the day."

"Scrubbed?" Michael Shannon, the team's catcher, echoed. "Frank's our number-one pitcher!"

"Yeah," came the complaints of the other players. "And Joe . . ."

Coach Tarkanian silenced his team with a steely glare.

"Why are we scrubbed?" Frank asked. "It couldn't be because of bad grades. We're both good students."

"It isn't grades," Coach Tarkanian said. "Just go." The coach turned to the other players. "Novick," he said to the team's number-two starting pitcher, "get to the bullpen and get warmed up. Gitenstein, you'll take Joe's spot."

The team once more muttered their protests, but the discussion was closed. Frank and Joe left the dugout and headed for the locker room. Both were bewildered and very upset. When they reached the locker room, Officer Con Riley was waiting for them.

"Con?" Joe asked. "What's going on?"

"Has there been a break in the jewelry case?" Frank asked.

"In a way," Con said sadly. "Look, I hate to do this, but, Frank and Joe Hardy, you are both under arrest."

14 Frank and Joe Go to Jail

"Oh, now this seems familiar," Joe said.

"It's not as if we didn't expect it."

"What was that, Frank?" Con asked.

"I think we'll go with the right to remain silent for now," Frank replied.

Riley read the brothers their Miranda Rights.

"You are being arrested for robbing Bayport Midtown Furriers," Con said. "Do you wish to make a confession at this time?"

"Furriers? Not a jewelry store?" Frank was a little confused.

"Uh, we do not wish to make any statements," Joe said. Frank nodded his agreement.

"Just sticking to procedure," Con said. He allowed them to change out of their uniforms.

"Con," Frank said as the man led them out to

his patrol car, "thanks for doing this yourself. I mean it. I know you'll stick by us."

Con smiled. "I'll get you through booking as swiftly as possible. I've already arranged for your father to meet us at the station. It's bending procedure, but I'm willing to take a risk for you two."

At the local precinct house, Con proved true to his word. The Hardy brothers were rushed through booking and led to an interrogation room. Con stayed with them the entire time. Soon Chief Collig, Fenton Hardy, and Brady Stelfreeze joined them.

"Well, well," Collig said with a smirk. "I'm a bit surprised, I have to admit."

"Glad to make your day," Joe said.

"Let's just roll the evidence," Collig said. "That should speed up a confession."

"I will note comments like that as coercion and duress," Stelfreeze warned.

Con went to a television console and pressed Play on the video machine. The screen lit up and displayed a scene taken from the Midtown Furriers' security camera. It plainly showed Joe and Frank entering a side door of the furriers' warehouse, finding some boxes of furs, and loading them into a truck through the loading-dock door.

Frank leaned over to whisper to his brother. "The furs are a switch. But they didn't take much effort to alter the tape."

"What was that?" Chief Collig asked. Frank did not reply. "Suit yourself," Collig said. "Anyway, we don't need a confession."

"We plan to show how that tape is faulty evidence," Stelfreeze said. "We will show that it has been tampered with."

"Oh, we don't plan to hang this all on the tape," Collig said. "Con?"

Con Riley threw a plastic bag on the table in plain sight of everyone gathered there. Inside was a ragged swatch of fur.

"We got a search warrant for your van, based on the tape. We searched it while you were in school. We found this under the passenger seat."

"We've been set up!" Joe yelled.

"Simmer down," Stelfreeze instructed him. Suddenly there was a knock at the door.

"Yeah?" Collig shouted. A uniformed officer opened the door and poked his head inside the interrogation room.

"I have papers signed by Judge Bone, authorizing release on bail of Frank and Joe Hardy."

Brady Stelfreeze smiled.

"When you hire the best, you get the best results," Fenton Hardy said.

Chief Collig shook his head with disappointment. "Get on out of here," he said. "For now, anyway."

Joe and Frank stood up. Stelfreeze, their father,

and Con Riley filed through the door and out of the room. Frank and Joe started to follow them.

"Hey," Collig said softly, "for what it's worth, I don't like being the bad cop right now. I hope you guys are being framed."

Frank and Joe nodded their heads and smiled.

When they got outside, Fenton Hardy drove up in his sons' van.

"It was in impound," he said. "Stelfreeze got it released." Frank and Joe got in the van.

"You want to drive?" Fenton asked Joe.

"Nah, you go ahead," he replied. "Hey, where's your car?"

"I came here with Stelfreeze. We're going to meet him at our house for a strategy session. Maybe you two want to bring me up to speed."

Frank and Joe filled their father in on their involvement with what they referred to as the *Monty Mania* case. They walked him through their encounters with Monty, their interactions with Rojas and Wingfoot, their girlfriends' involvement, and each of the theories they had put forward on the case.

"Wow," Fenton said, "that's a busy handful of days. So what you believe is that this hypnotist is planting posthypnotic suggestions in his guests' minds, while Ronald Johnson uses his control of the security company to pull off these robberies and frame somebody else."

"That's pretty much it at this point," Frank said.

"Monty has people do stuff on stage that is easily morphed into the security camera footage. And Johnson set up each store's security system, so he would have no problem bypassing it. Then to cover the scent of its being an inside job, he trips the alarms when he's ready to make a getaway."

"But even if you run all of the videotapes through your computer and show how Johnson could have framed everybody, it still doesn't prove anything. Especially now that some hard evidence has been found in your van."

"Yeah, how did that get in here?" Frank asked.

"Probably when we were tussling with the thugs-of-the-week club," Joe said. "I thought that whole tangle ended a bit too easily."

"Well, now we just have to catch Johnson in the act," Frank said. "The missing goods have to be tracked right to his door."

"That's a tall order, son," Fenton said. "But if it can be done, you guys will do it."

After a long night of legal strategizing, the brothers finally got to bed just before midnight.

The next morning they decided to be late for school so they could check out Eye Spy Security. They figured a bold front-door approach would serve them best.

"Put on a nice shirt and a tie," Frank suggested as he and Joe got dressed.

Joe winced. "I hate ties. Why a tie?"

"It will give our appearance at the Eye Spy Security corporate offices a bit more legitimacy."

When they reached the office, they walked straight into the reception area.

"May I help you?" asked a young woman sitting behind a desk.

Joe smiled. He gave his brother an I'll-handle-this look. "Yes, you certainly can," he said as he approached the desk. "We represent a local group of investors who . . ."

Frank tuned out his brother's smooth talk, choosing instead to wander around the reception area. He made his way close to the entrance to the interior offices. Through a set of double glass doors, he saw a familiar face.

"Bill," he said as he opened the door. "How's it going?"

The security installation man Frank had met at the Bayport Jewelry Exchange gave the teen a puzzled look. Then a smile crossed his face.

"Hey, kid," he said. "It's going well. What are you doing around here?"

Frank walked up to the installation man.

"All right, I'll confess," Frank whispered. "I'm here to learn how to foil Eye Spy's latest security system." Then he flashed the man a big smile.

Bill laughed. "That's a good one. But, hey, are you here looking for a job maybe? I could put in a word for you."

"It's a tempting offer," Frank said. "But I don't know—installing alarms at jewelry stores every day? Sounds like it could get old."

"Hey, we don't just do jewels. In fact, I'm headed out to do a repair at a fur warehouse."

Just then Bill's beeper chimed. "I got to get this," he said. Bill turned around and walked down the hallway.

Frank looked around. He spotted an open office door and decided to peek inside. Nobody was in the office, so Frank made sure the coast was clear in the hall and then he walked over to the desk. On top was a stack of papers—bills, from what Frank could gather. The one on top was for Diamonds and Pearls Jewelers. Frank took a closer look and could see the impression of something handwritten reflected on the bill, as if it had been under a piece of paper on which somebody had written a note.

Frank held the paper up to the light.

"Next?" he read.

Just then there was noise in the hallway. Frank put the paper down on the desk and walked into the hall.

"Hey, what are you doing?" asked a man, whom Frank recognized as Ronald Johnson.

"Uh, I'm looking to set up some security for my dad's new art gallery," Frank replied.

"Art gallery, huh?" Johnson said, approaching

Frank. "Well, I'm Ronald Johnson, president here at Eye Spy Security. You've certainly come to the right place for all your security needs."

Frank shook Johnson's extended hand.

"Now, if you'll just head on down the hall to the left, I'll have one of our security experts show you some of our wonderful systems and set up an appointment to have one of our men survey the gallery."

"Great," Frank said as he walked off in the direction in which Johnson had pointed. He had wanted to press the conversation with Johnson further, but he could tell that the man was not going to stand there and be questioned.

After Frank was certain Johnson had left the hallway, he turned around and went back to the reception area. Joe was leaning against the receptionist's desk, still smiling and talking. Frank tapped Joe on the shoulder.

"Let's get going," he said. Joe hesitated. Frank gently pulled on his sleeve.

"Well, thanks," Joe said over his shoulder to the receptionist as Frank dragged him toward the exit. "I'll keep all that in mind."

"Keep what in mind?" Frank asked as they got in the elevator.

"Nothing," Joe answered. "Just small talk."

Frank snorted and shook his head. "I had some small talk, too. With our main suspect."

"Wow," Joe said. "I'm impressed."

"Don't be. I didn't get anything."

They exited the building and headed for the van. Suddenly, the normal sounds of downtown traffic were pierced by the squeal of grinding brakes.

"Oh, great," Joe said as he pointed at a black sedan. The car was cutting across three lanes of traffic to make a U-turn. "Here we go again."

15 Evasive Maneuvers

"When will these guys ever give up?" Frank moaned as he sprinted for the van. Joe headed out into the street and ran for the driver's side of the vehicle. When both Hardys were in the van, Joe started the engine.

He could see the sedan in the mirror.

"They're a few cars back," Joe said. "Good thing there's some traffic." Joe saw a few inches of daylight between the two cars about to pass the van. He threw the van into gear and shot out into traffic just as the first car passed. In the other car the brakes were slammed on and the horn was pushed.

The van was free of its parking spot and Joe accelerated into the downtown traffic. Frank looked out the passenger-side window.

"They're passing traffic on the right," he said. "They'll be able to slip in behind us."

"Great! A slow-speed chase through traffic. That's exciting." Joe made a right turn onto a side street, hoping to find some space to gain speed. His instinct was rewarded; the traffic was sparse on the narrow side street.

"Let's lose these guys," Frank said as he spotted the sedan making the right also.

"Yeah, I don't want to dance with these goons again. I want to get to chemistry class."

Joe pushed the accelerator to the floor. He came right up behind a slow-moving family car before he pulled the wheel to the left. He drove the van across the double yellow line into oncoming traffic. At the last possible second, in the face of the oncoming honking cars, Joe jerked the steering wheel to the right and slipped the van in front of the family car. He could hear the screech of brakes behind him. A glance in the rearview mirror revealed that the sedan had failed to pull off the same maneuver.

"Light's going yellow," Frank warned.

Joe eased off the gas a little, forcing the cars behind him to slow down as they approached the intersection. When the light turned red, Joe punched the gas and made a sharp left. The sedan was stuck behind the family car at the red light.

"Three for three," Joe said. "These two better go back to bad guy school."

"What do you expect?" Frank asked. "They've had it easy. Monty Andrews and Ronald Johnson set up simple, foolproof heists to pull. They probably haven't had to do much thinking."

After finishing morning classes, Frank and Joe met the rest of the gang for lunch. They filled everyone in on what had happened, and then they revealed their plan.

"We need to catch these guys with the stolen goods. That is, assuming they haven't fenced them yet," Chet suggested.

"Con said that none of the stuff has turned up anywhere," Frank said. "With luck, it's still stashed somewhere here in town."

"Here's what we're going to do," Joe said. Everybody huddled over the table to go over the plan. "It'll take all of us to pull it off."

Later that evening everyone was in position. Frank and Joe sat in the van, parked around the corner from Diamonds and Pearls Jewelers. It was nearly nine o'clock, and the store was closing for the night. As they watched the owner of the store lock the front door, the cellular phone rang.

"Talk to me," Frank said, answering the phone.

"It's Tony. We've got a sighting on Monty Andrews. He's leaving the studio."

"Stick with him," Frank said.

Tony, Chet, Iola, and Callie had been assigned

to keep an eye on the performer; none of them wanted to be left out of the manhunt, and it was probably safer to go in large numbers anyway. They still suspected that he might be deeply involved with the robberies. "We need to know if he heads our way."

"What's up at your end?" Tony asked.

"We have the store staked out. It just closed. If Monty plans to rob this place, it'll probably take him twenty minutes to get here. By then the area will be pretty vacant."

Frank hung up the phone. Thirty minutes later it rang again.

"It's Chet. Monty stopped for dinner."

"Maybe he doesn't do the job himself," Joe said.

Joe tapped his brother's arm. Frank looked through the front windshield. He spotted two large, familiar figures walking up the street toward Diamonds and Pearls.

"Why do it himself when he has those two goons," Frank said. "We'll be in touch," he said into the phone. "It's show time."

Joe and Frank watched as the two thugs spent a moment at the front door of the store. When they had disappeared inside, Joe started up the engine.

"Let them get the goods," Frank said. "Then we'll nail them."

The brothers waited a few minutes. The two thugs left the store from the front door and nonchalantly walked down the street. They turned the corner opposite from where Frank and Joe sat. Then suddenly, the air was filled with the sound of Diamonds and Pearls' alarm.

"Hit it," Frank ordered.

Joe threw the van into gear just as the familiar black sedan came roaring up the block.

"Great," Joe said. "We guessed wrong on which direction they might go. I thought for sure they'd head downtown. They've already seen us."

"I don't care," Frank said. "We've got to run these guys to ground before they can get rid of the goods."

"Wait," Joe said as he kept pace with the accelerating sedan. "Forget the goods from this one store. Let's see if we can catch them with everything. Then we'll all be cleared of the charges."

"Good thinking," Frank said. "But if they know we're on their tail, they probably won't go to their hideout."

"Then we'll let them lose us. Call Callie and have her intercept their trail. When the thugs think they're in the clear, they won't be looking for our backup crew. Callie can follow them to the stash."

Frank placed the call. Joe kept pace with the sedan, which led them in vague circles around town. When Callie confirmed that she had picked up the trail, Joe dropped back and let the sedan make a sharp right turn. Joe drove straight.

"Oops," he said. "We lost them."

"We got them," Chet said through the cellular phone. "They're heading for the outskirts of town on Mill Road. Take Peach Street and you should be able to make a left and get behind us."

Joe followed Chet's directions. He hung back on Peach Street until he spotted the sedan and Callie's car pass. He waited another minute before he made a left onto Mill Road.

"We don't see you," Frank said into the phone.

"Left onto Lirica Lane. It's a side street about a mile from Peach. Okay, they just made a right down an unmarked dirt road. We can see some lights in the distance, maybe a house."

"Don't do anything until we get there," Frank said. "Meet us on Lirica." Frank clicked off the phone. Joe made the left onto Lirica Lane. He spotted Callie's car pulled off to the side of the road. He pulled the van up behind the car.

"Okay, where are Chet and Iola?" Frank asked as he got out of the van.

"Those boneheads walked down the dirt path toward the house," Tony replied. "We told them to wait."

"Oh, great," Joe said. "We'd better try to catch them before they get into trouble."

The four friends jogged down the dirt path. As they neared the house, they slowed and walked very quietly. The black sedan was parked in front of a small brown house. The car was empty. Joe spotted Chet and Iola crouching next to the car. Suddenly the siblings stood up and walked around the side of the house. Joe wanted to holler for them to stop, but that kind of noise would certainly blow their cover.

Frank shook his head. He used his hand to signal the group silently to stay low and follow him. They all crept stealthily forward and knelt down beside the sedan.

Joe peeked above the hood of the car and focused on the front window of the house. He could see movement inside. The occupants of the house were moving from the front room out of sight. A minute later there were four figures inside the house. Joe recognized two in particular.

"Oh, man," he said, slumping to the ground. "Why doesn't anybody ever follow instructions?"

16 Break In, Break Out

"Don't tell me," Frank said. "They have Chet and Iola."

Joe nodded. "They're all in the front room," he whispered. "Iola and Chet are standing close together. Zybysko's got a gun on them."

"Well, that cinches it," Frank said. "I want to get in there before they get tied to chairs or something."

"Yeah," Joe responded. "We may need Chet's muscle. So, one more tangle with our favorite thugs."

"What?" Callie whispered, not believing what she had just heard.

"We have to go in there," Frank said. "We have to keep those goons from doing anything Chet and Iola won't live to regret."

"How do we get in there?" Tony asked.

"'We' don't," Joe said. "Just me and Frank."

Callie and Tony began to protest.

"You guys have to alert the police," Joe said. "Go back to the car and use the cell phone."

"Shouldn't I stay here to back you guys up?" Tony asked.

"We need police backup for this," Frank said. "And I don't want to put anybody else in the line of fire."

Callie began to protest again, but Frank shushed her. Reluctantly, Callie and Tony made their way back to the car.

"Where fools rush in?" Joe asked.

"Age before beauty," Frank said as he stood up and headed for the front door.

"Hello in there!" he called out as Joe followed behind him. "We've come to call a truce."

The brothers approached the front door.

"Come on, guys," Joe shouted. "It's just us."

A tan face appeared at the window. Then it disappeared and the front door opened.

"Get inside," Zybysko said, pointing a gun in Frank's face.

"Take it easy," Frank said as he entered the house with his hands up. Joe put his hands up and came in also. The tan thug closed the door.

"You guys really can't stay away from this?" Spicolli asked. Instead of the usually ill-thought-out suit, Spicolli wore a green paisley shirt and striped slacks.

"I just can't let you walk around like that," Joe said. "I came to take you shopping."

"Enough of your wisecracks," Spicolli said. He backhanded Joe in the face. Joe sprawled back against the couch.

"Joe!" Iola cried.

Zybysko trained his gun on the girl. Chet took two steps forward and stood protectively in front of his sister.

"Everybody calm down," Frank said. "Look, these two have nothing to do with any of this," he said, indicating Chet and Iola. "Let them go."

"Good try," Zybysko said. "We're not stupid. If they walk out of here, they'll bring the cops."

Joe stood up and held his hand to his chin. "So I guess that means we're as good as dead."

"Oh, that's good, give the bad guys some ideas," Chet said.

"All I mean is," Joe said, "if you plan to kill us, the least you can do is fill us in on some of the details. You guys have had us chasing our tails since these robberies started. You might as well let us die with some good answers."

"Fair enough," Spicolli said. "Ask away."

"How'd you get tied up with Monty Andrews?" Frank asked.

"That goof? He's an unwitting accomplice. He's

in so deep to Ronald Johnson, he'd dress like a duck if we told him to."

"So Johnson's pulling the strings," Joe said.

"He sets them up," Zybysko boasted, "and we knock them down."

"Sounds good," Frank said, but Joe could tell his brother was listening to something else other than his captor's comments. Joe smiled.

"What the— Sirens!" Zybysko yelled. He ran to the window. As he passed between Joe and Frank, both brothers stuck out their legs. The thug tripped and flew headfirst into the window, shattering the glass.

"Hey!" Spicolli shouted as he pointed his gun on Joe. His attention distracted for a moment, Spicolli failed to see the lamp that smashed against his face. He crumpled to the floor.

"Enough with the guns already," Iola said as she kicked the firearm toward the other side of the room.

"Good work, Sis," Chet said. He went to the window and kicked the other gun out of Zybysko's reach.

Just then the front door burst open and several police officers charged into the house.

"When are you guys going to learn some stealth?" Frank asked Con Riley.

"Who needs stealth with you two on the case?" Con smirked. "We're just here to mop up after you."

"Well, there's quite a bit of mopping to do," Joe said. He filled Con in on the goons' confession while the other officers handcuffed them and carted them away.

"If you lean hard enough, they might give up some evidence on Ronald Johnson," Frank said. "Otherwise they'll do all the time for their boss's crime."

"Also," Joe added, "you should arrest Monty Andrews as an accessory. That should scare him enough to get him to testify against Johnson."

"Will do," replied Con. "Any more arrest warrants you want issued?"

"Can you arrest Ronald Johnson?" Joe asked.

"Not yet," Con answered. "This Ronald Johnson is some character. He's put so many layers between himself and the actual crimes that he has a good chance of walking away scot-free. It's good to be the boss."

"You can't let him get away with all of this!" Frank exclaimed.

"Oh, we'll get him," Con said with a smile. "We'll put so much heat on these two goons and on Monty Andrews that they'll testify against Johnson just so they can all have another roommate in jail."

After the police got Spicolli and Zybysko into a police cruiser, they searched the house. It didn't take them very long to find the huge stash of jewelry and furs that had been stolen over the past week.

"It's good work if you can get it," one of the officers said as he presented the valuables to Con.

"You'll all have to come down to make statements," Con said to the teenagers.

"Can we do it tonight?" Joe asked. "We have a baseball game to play tomorrow. We missed opening day."

Con laughed and led everybody out of the house.

The next day Frank was in his Bayport High baseball uniform, taking his warm-up throws from the pitcher's mound at Shoreham High. Roberto Rojas and Pepper Wingfoot, flanked by the whole Shoreham baseball team, walked out to the mound. Rojas was wielding a baseball bat.

Joe, fearing that his brother was in trouble, ran onto the diamond.

"Back off, guys," Joe said as he got side by side with Frank.

"Hey, there's no trouble here," Rojas said. "We have something for you guys."

Wingfoot held up a baseball. "This is for you, Frank," he said. "We know you put yourselves on the line to clear us of robbery. We wanted to say thanks."

Frank took the ball. He saw that it was autographed by the whole Shoreham team.

"And this bat is for you, Slugger," Rojas said, handing an autographed bat to Joe. "It took us sixteen innings, but without you two in the game, we beat Bayport on opening day."

"Then you won't mind if we whip you guys today," Joe said.

"Give it your best shot," replied Wingfoot as the Shoreham players headed toward their dugout. "Give it your best shot."